NORTH

RTH

Donna Jo Napoli

GREENWILLOW BOOKS
An Imprint of HarperCollins*Publishers*

The text of this book is set in Mrs. Eaves.
Map copyright © 2004 by Elena Furrow
Book design by Chad W. Beckerman

Library of Congress Cataloging-in-Publication Data
Napoli, Donna Jo.
North / by Donna Jo Napoli.
p. cm.
"Greenwillow Books."
Summary: Tired of his mother's overprotectiveness and
intrigued by the life of African American explorer Matthew
Henson, twelve-year-old Alvin travels north and spends a
season with a trapper near the Arctic Circle.
ISBN 0-06-057987-0 (trade).
ISBN 0-06-057988-9 (lib. bdg.)
[1. Runaways—Fiction. 2. Inuit—Fiction. 3. Voyages and
travels—Fiction. 4. Bylot Island (Nunavut)—Fiction.
5. Eskimos—Fiction. 6. Canada—Fiction. 7. Henson, Matthew
Alexander, 1866–1955—Fiction.] I. Title.
PZ7.N15Nr 2004 [Fic]—dc22 2003011121

First Edition 10 9 8 7 6 5 4 3 2

 GREENWILLOW BOOKS

For Nina White, with love

Thanks to Jasmine Boddie, Brenda Bowen, Jean Briggs, Caitlyn Dlouhy, Ralph Fasold, Wendy Lamb, Susan Lipsett, Jeannine Lee, Alice Martin, Diane Martin, Sabrina Martinez, Ethel Moore, Nick Nichols, Ramneek Pooni, Hillard Pouncy, Joe Razza, Britt Riley, Margaret Robinson, Judy Schachner, Fiona Simpson, Stephanie Strassel, Ann Taylor, Richard Tchen, Gill Vandervluct, Jennifer Weiss, Fred Wherry, Jennifer Wingertzahn, Tony Williamson, Jeff Wu, and Gilbert Youmans, all of whom dutifully plowed through early drafts. And thanks to Keren Rice, for supplying me with Canadian publications, and Laura Talbot, for making me a video of Canadian winter life. A thank-you to a linguistic informant who wishes to remain unnamed, but who helped me keep straight the various varieties of Inuktitut, as well as gave me invaluable comments on the story.

Thanks to Celeste McLaughlin's fifth-grade class at the Swarthmore-Rutledge School in 1997–98. Thanks to Alex Fitzpatrick's and George King's sixth-grade classes at the Evans Computer Magnet School in 1999–2000. Thanks to Ellen Gidaro's fifth-grade class at the Swarthmore-Rutledge School in 2001–2002.

Thanks especially to my whole family, and to the memory of my mother. This is the last manuscript of mine that she read.

And, most of all, thanks to Rebecca Davis and Virginia Duncan, my wonderful editors.

Contents

CHAPTER ONE

Back to School

Alvin stood at the window and looked through the bars. The sidewalk outside was still empty. If he hurried, he could get to school before everyone else. He wouldn't have to talk to anyone about Christmas.

The steam kettle screeched. Alvin ran into the kitchen and turned it off. He could do without hot chocolate. It was more important to avoid the other kids. And Grandma would use the hot water to make tea anyway, so he hadn't wasted the gas. He grabbed his new backpack with one hand and his jacket with the other and ran for the door.

"Get that coat on, Alvin," his mother called from her bedroom. There was no way she could see him.

"How does she always know?" he muttered.

"The mamma knows," said Grandma. She was sitting on the couch in the dark.

"Grandma, what you doing there?"

"Taking a rest. Get your jacket on or your mamma won't be happy."

A rest in the morning? How long had Grandma been up? "I don't care," he said, even as he pulled the jacket on.

"Yes, you do, boy. If the mamma ain't happy, ain't nobody happy." Grandma laughed. She loved that saying: If the mamma ain't happy, ain't nobody happy. She gave Mamma a sweatshirt with that saying on it for the fourth day of Kwanzaa. Mamma didn't love it as much as Grandma did, especially since she hated words like *ain't*. But she wore it to sleep in, because Grandma had bought it at a store on Mount Pleasant Street that sold only goods made by African-American–owned businesses. So the sweatshirt was a symbol of a Kwanzaa principle—as Grandma put it, "You buy from me and I'll buy from you." Mamma believed Kwanzaa was one of the good things that had happened to black people in her lifetime. Grandma didn't care one way or the other about Kwanzaa, but she was ready to take advantage of anything that would allow her a belly laugh.

Alvin zipped up his jacket, kissed Grandma quick on the cheek, and left.

It was only a few blocks to Bancroft Elementary. The morning was pretty cold, but not what it should have been for January in Washington, D.C. The gibbons at the zoo, just six blocks away, screamed good morning to one another in high voices that echoed all over Mount Pleasant. He loved the zoo. Someday he'd go to the Asian jungles where the gibbons lived free. And he'd go to the Amazon, and Africa, too.

Yeah, especially Africa. He'd go to Africa first, because the last book he'd read on primates said the gorillas were threatened with extinction. No more gorillas. Intelligent, gentle beasts, gone.

Alvin pulled up the collar of his jacket and jammed his hands into his pockets. He walked with his eyes glued to the sidewalk.

The dog behind the wood fence on Park Road barked wildly. Alvin ran half a block before his heart slowed again. He knew the fence was tall, but it never reassured him enough. He was afraid of dogs. None of his friends owned one.

"That you, Alvin?" called Shastri.

Alvin kept walking without looking around.

"Hey, Dwarf, that you?"

Shastri's footsteps got louder. Alvin stopped and waited.

"What's the rush?" Shastri came up beside him.

Alvin had to make three steps for every two of Shastri's. He looked up at his best friend, the friend he'd been avoiding since Christmas Day. "Hi."

"We'll get there early, going at this hour. I couldn't believe that was you I saw from the window. I had to stuff my toast in my mouth."

"Sorry," Alvin muttered.

"'S okay. You're not going to believe this. I got it. I got the mountain bike."

Alvin knew Shastri would have gotten it. He tried to smile.

"It's perfect. Cold blue. It can go anywhere. You got to come see it."

"Yeah," said Alvin. They were at the school doors now. Luckily, Alvin and Shastri weren't in the same classes this year; at least he wouldn't have to listen to this all day long. "I got to go," said Alvin, "I got something to do."

"Cool." Shastri gave a quick nod. "After school?"

Alvin waved and went to his classroom, willing himself not to let jealousy get the better of him.

The thing was, Alvin needed a mountain bike,

actually needed it. Uncle Pete had promised to take him on a bike trip over spring break if Mamma bought it. A trip through Maryland, past farms, through woods. Camping the whole way. Like pioneers.

Uncle Pete used to take Alvin camping when he lived here. But he'd gotten a job in Philadelphia two years ago and moved away. He came back for a weekend a few times a year. And Alvin had visited him in June. Mamma had ridden up on the train with him, and Uncle Pete had ridden back with him. The whole way they'd talked about plans for the bike trip.

When Alvin told Shastri he was dreaming about a mountain bike, Shastri started dreaming too. Alvin didn't say anything more about it—the bike and the trip became Alvin's private hope, sacred almost. But Shastri started wanting that bike so much that he could hardly talk about anything else. And look what happened—Shastri got the bike and Alvin didn't.

And Shastri didn't even need his. His parents took him to all kinds of new places.

A bike. With a bike, Alvin wouldn't have needed anyone to take him anywhere. He could have gone on his own.

CHAPTER TWO

The Project

Ms. Artiga stood at the front of the room and asked up and down the aisles what each person liked best about the holidays. And they answered, with stupid, happy grins on their faces. Things. That's what everyone talked about. All the things they got. Except Jasmine. She went to Disney World in Orlando, Florida. Lucky Jasmine.

And then there was Malik. Malik sat silent a moment and looked at Ms. Artiga with his neck sort of sunk in on itself—he seemed like a turtle peeking out of its shell. "We don't get nothing till . . . "

Ms. Artiga cleared her throat.

Malik blinked and started over. "We don't get

anything till January sixth." He glanced around with a challenge on his face. "The Epiphany."

Alvin felt suddenly lucky to be sitting behind Malik. Malik's answer had stirred up so much commotion that when Ms. Artiga turned to Alvin, he figured he had a chance of sliding through. He said quickly, "What I liked best was not coming to school." Everyone gave a surprised laugh. Alvin had a reputation for working hard at school. Too hard. Whatever, their laughter did the trick: Ms. Artiga let it go.

Good. Because he didn't want to talk about the things Mamma had given him—the backpack and the handmade books and the CD of African drum songs and the wool hat that was big on him, so that it would last a few years. He liked that stuff, especially the drum songs—Mamma knew he'd been eyeing that CD—but he didn't want to talk about them because what was really on his mind was the mountain bike he hadn't gotten.

It wasn't that Alvin had expected to get it. He hadn't. He and Mamma had argued about it. Mamma said no one really needed a bike in the city, mountain or any other kind. Alvin had said he'd pay for it himself, but Mamma shook her head. She said it was dangerous—you shouldn't ride on the sidewalk because that's where people were, and you shouldn't ride in the street because that's where cars were, and you shouldn't ride in Rock Creek Park because that's where perverts were. Mamma knew all about Rock Creek Park because she worked for the Park Service—inspecting paths, picking up litter, investigating calls about hurt animals. When Alvin was little, he used to go to work with Mamma. He'd pretend he was an explorer in the wilderness. And whenever he found Mamma a bird nest, she'd squeal with delight and hug him close. Mamma collected bird nests.

Anyway, a bike didn't make sense to Mamma. Just like Rollerblades didn't make sense to her, and a skateboard didn't make sense to her.

And part of it was the money. Mamma worked so hard. She came home most nights totally beat. Alvin knew Mamma couldn't afford to lay out a big lump of money for a mountain bike. That's why he'd offered to pay for it himself. He'd been working for that bike since Uncle Pete first suggested the trip. From June to September, he'd helped neighbors clean out their basements, and he'd weeded old Mrs. Ford's vegetable garden all the way through the end of October. He still had a job every Saturday morning sweeping her front stoop. He had saved $439. More than enough for the bike in case Mamma didn't get it for him for Christmas.

Then what had happened? Exactly what Alvin would have predicted if he hadn't let himself get so carried away by the fantasy: She hadn't bought it and she'd forbidden him to buy it for himself. It didn't matter who paid for it. No.

For as long as he could remember, Mamma had said no. Other kids went places and did things that were normal to them. But for Alvin those things were privileges he gaped at, like a four-year-old wishing he could do the big-boy things. Ordinary things—as ordinary as going on an overnight at your best friend's. He got good at making up excuses why he couldn't go, so no one would know his mother kept him home.

But they knew anyway. Or at least Shastri did. Well, sure. That's why he didn't even ask Alvin if he'd gotten the bike this morning. That was it. He didn't want to embarrass him. Just like Alvin would never embarrass Shastri by talking in front of other kids about all the expensive toys Shastri had.

No. No bike. No way.

So Alvin didn't expect that bike on Christmas

morning. He'd just kind of hoped, in that sort of pretend way you do when you know you can't really have something.

Alvin would spend spring break reading about other places and never going there. He drummed his fingers on the underside of his desk.

When Ms. Artiga finished asking the last kid, she said, "I'm glad you had such wonderful holidays. But we have to buckle down now, because I have a treat. Oh, you're going to love this."

Someone snickered. Alvin knew it was just for show, though. When Ms. Artiga said they were going to love something, they usually did. He sat up straighter.

Ms. Artiga walked along the sunny side of the room, carrying a stack of books in one arm and propping them up one by one on the windowsills as she spoke. "I borrowed a bunch of books from the central library downtown for our next project. February is the month we look at the history of African Americans."

"But this is January," said Malik.

"Right. So it's time to prepare for February. Each of you is going to find out about a famous African American. There are plenty of books up here. I want you to pick one and start reading right away, because you have to finish it by the end of next week. That's your secondary research."

"Secondary?" asked Sharee. "What's that mean?"

"It means you're reading what other people have found out. But—now give me your full attention— the wonderful part of this project is that you'll do primary research, too. Next year you'll be at Deal Junior High, and you've got to be ready." Ms. Artiga slapped her fist into the palm of her hand. "So once you've finished reading your book—your secondary research—it's time for primary research. You have to discover something on your own about your hero."

"Or heroine," said Chanelle.

"Right."

"But what if we pick someone dead?" asked Alicia.

"That's okay. Inside each book I put a suggestion about primary research for that particular person. You might visit a museum that has something that belonged to that person—so you can see it with your own eyes. You might write to that person's descendants and ask how that person affected their lives. You might try to have an experience that person had—so you can feel it for yourself." Ms. Artiga rubbed her hands together. "Okay, now please get up quietly and walk in a line past the books, so you can see all of them before you choose. And choose wisely, because you're going to make a report about your hero—or heroine—and present it to the class during February. The best report will get a prize."

"What prize?" asked Tramaine.

"I haven't decided yet. But you're going to love it."

"I pick Rosa Parks," said Chanelle.

"No one's picking yet," said Ms. Artiga.

Alvin was disappointed. Like Chanelle, he already knew who he wanted. He knew from the minute Ms. Artiga said the word *hero*.

"After you've seen all the books, I'll hold each one up and if more than one person wants it, we'll draw straws." Ms. Artiga rubbed her hands together again, then clasped them tight. "Nothing is more empowering than primary research, because you learn through your own experience—so you truly understand, and you never forget."

They filed past the books. Alvin searched book after book. Ms. Artiga was smart—she had to have included his hero. She had to.

Then he found it—a cover with a mustached man in the middle of the Arctic snow, smiling like the empty, wild world around him was perfect. He read the title: *Matthew Henson, North Pole Explorer*. Alvin already knew a lot about Henson. This book was new to him, though. When Ms. Artiga held it up, he had to draw straws with Chuck. Chuck wanted George Washington Carver as his second choice, but Alvin had no second choice. His hand shook as he picked the straw—then he let out a little whoop of joy.

CHAPTER THREE

Winning

After school, Alvin walked home with Shastri. Tramaine passed them. "How's it going?" he said.

Alvin was too startled to answer. Tramaine didn't usually talk to people like Alvin and Shastri. He had an older brother, and they hung out a lot with kids Alvin didn't know.

"All right," said Shastri.

"What I liked best was not coming to school," said Tramaine, mimicking the way Alvin had said those words to Ms. Artiga that morning. He laughed. "Cool, young bull." He gave a wave and crossed the street.

"Looks like you've got a new friend," said Shastri.

Alvin didn't answer. But he felt light and happy—almost elated. He'd never been good at quick joking or clever answers. Maybe he was changing. Maybe he would earn himself a new nickname—something better than Dwarf.

They went into Shastri's house through the rear door and fixed themselves deviled ham sandwiches. The meat came all chopped up and perfectly spiced in a little can the right size for two sandwiches. Shastri had deviled ham almost every day after school, but for Alvin it was a treat. Canned meat was expensive, and Mamma never bought it.

"Ready?" Shastri went into the front hall and came back through the kitchen, rolling his bike. He stopped so Alvin could inspect it.

Alvin pressed both thumbs on a tire. "Good tires."

"Tubeless," said Shastri. "And the frame's carbon."

Carbon was stiffer than aluminum. Sturdier. Alvin looked at the shock springs on front and back. He ran his hand over the handlebars and the con- toured seat. This bike was made for hard travel.

They went outside in silence, not meeting each other's eyes. Shastri rode up and down the block, then disappeared around the corner. When he circled home, he stopped and held the bike out for Alvin.

Alvin's throat was so thick, his "thanks" came out croaky. He rode around the block three times. The bike had quick steering. He loved the way it bounced over the potholes in the street. He loved everything about it.

When he handed over the bike, he managed to say clearly, "Good bike." After all, if he couldn't have a mountain bike, he was glad his best friend could, at least.

"Yeah," said Shastri. "Thanks. Help me break it in, okay? I'll ride. Then you'll ride. After school every day."

"Sounds good." And it did. It really did. Good old Shastri. Alvin felt a thousand times better.

Shastri rolled the bike back into the front hall. Then he let Alvin sit down at his computer while he went into the living room to practice piano.

Alvin typed in matthewhenson.com. It worked. Within the next half hour he'd found a site about the Arlington memorial. And he'd found out tons more about Henson. Matthew Henson had had three wives. He had married a woman and divorced her when she had a child with another man while he was on an expedition. Next he married Lucy Ross, and he had no children with her. Then, in the middle of an expedition, he took an Eskimo wife in Greenland. They didn't have a wedding ceremony—and it wouldn't have been legal, anyway, because he was still married to Lucy. But they had a child. One son.

Anaquak Henson was born in 1906.

And Anaquak had five children. All boys. And they had children too.

Alvin looked at the computer screen, at the photo of Laila Henson, Matthew Henson's great-granddaughter. Her face turned to the camera with a beautiful, open smile. Her hands rested on her lap, fingers spread. Her hair hung down her back, glossy and thick. Alvin leaned back and stared at her.

Shastri was still practicing. He'd moved on from finger exercises to actual songs. He was good, and from the way he was playing, Alvin guessed that he was happy. Alvin knew a little about music himself—about the way it could make you feel peaceful. He used to play the pennywhistle.

In fourth grade, recorder lessons at school had started. Every fourth grader in the city had to take lessons, and the school supplied the recorders. Alvin's was yellow. It stayed at school, with his name on masking tape stuck around the bottom rim. At the end of the year, the recorders were cleaned—and some new fourth grader got Alvin's the next fall. But for all of fourth grade, that yellow recorder was his.

Alvin easily learned the songs the music teacher assigned. Then Mr. Jackson told Alvin he had talent and he could come to the music room at recess for extra practice. So Alvin played new songs, sounding them out. Experimenting.

When he told Mrs. Sullivan, the librarian at the 16th Street public library, she found him a book of Duke Ellington scores. And she led him to the music carrel in the library, where he put on earphones and listened to CDs. He learned to play "Take the A Train." Then he discovered Louis Armstrong and his heart was stolen. His favorite song was "Georgia on My Mind."

One recess Mr. Jackson came into the music room as Alvin was playing "What a Wonderful World." That's when Mr. Jackson got the idea that Alvin could play the pennywhistle in the sixth graders' play about the American Revolution.

Mr. Jackson bought the pennywhistle brand-new. No one had used it the year before and the year before that and the year before that—not like the yellow recorder. The pennywhistle was narrow and shiny and it had a light, high, tinny sound. If Alvin blew hard, he could make the girls in the play shriek. But he only did that when Mr. Jackson was off somewhere else.

After the performance, Alvin wiped the pennywhistle on his shirt and gave it back to Mr. Jackson. That's how it had to be—the pennywhistle belonged to the school.

He should ask Mamma for a pennywhistle for his next birthday. That was a long way off, though—not till the end of summer. Instead, he could buy one for himself in that music store down in Adams Morgan—the one with the cool name: Madam's Organ. What else was he going to do with all that money he'd saved?

Everything suddenly seemed stupid and pointless. Alvin had saved money for a bike he'd never own. The best pennywhistle in the world couldn't make up for that. And no matter how peaceful a pennywhistle made him feel, it wasn't the same as how he'd feel on a mountain bike in the country. Or how Henson must have felt in the Arctic. No amount of riding Shastri's bike around the block was going to change that.

Alvin sat forward again and went from website to website, looking at lots of photographs of places in Canada that Henson had gone to and of things that Henson had used, like snowshoes and a parka, but he kept coming back to those photos of Laila. When he was walking home later, it struck him: He'd write to her, to Matthew Henson's great-granddaughter. That would be his primary research. That was one of Ms. Artiga's suggestions, after all, to write to a descendant of his hero. She'd write back to him, he was sure.

And he'd win the prize for the best project. He was sure of that, too.

CHAPTER FOUR

New Friends

That night Alvin read the book on Matthew Henson that he'd gotten from Ms. Artiga. It turned out better than he could have hoped, because it was full of things that Matthew Henson had actually said. When Alvin read them, he could hear Henson, could hear his deep, mellow voice practically crooning about the fierce beauty of the Arctic.

Fierce beauty. Alvin loved that phrase.

He read the book again, but this time only his favorite parts. And he memorized every detail he could.

At school he dazzled people with those details. He

hadn't intended to. In fact, it happened by accident. Tramaine came up to him in the lunch line and said, "Tell me something good."

And Alvin said, "Matthew Henson loved dogs." Immediately he wondered if that was true. All he really knew was that Henson wasn't afraid of dogs.

"Big deal," said Tramaine. "Little poodles?"

"Dogs on a dog team. Ferocious."

"All right," said Tramaine, drawing the words out over three syllables. "Pretty good." He growled like a dog and gave Alvin a tap on the back as though they were buddies.

Alvin hadn't said anything clever this time, but somehow he'd said the right thing. And his head filled with things to say the next time Tramaine came up to him.

He had to remember to include those very details in his project, because the prize was exactly what he wanted. Ms. Artiga had announced it that morning: The winner would get to help decide some of the activities for the sixth-grade field trip to Philadelphia in May. Last year the fifth-grade field trip had been to Williamsburg. Mamma wouldn't let him go, because the class had stayed overnight and she said he was too young for that. She didn't trust the chaperones to keep close enough watch. But if

Alvin was helping to decide the activities for the field trip this year, Mamma would have to let him go. She'd have to. He had to win that prize.

After school that same day, Tramaine and his brother and some third guy Alvin didn't know caught up with him and Shastri, and Tramaine said, "Got anything to tell my brother and all?"

"Everyone on the North Pole expeditions was white," said Alvin without hesitation, "everyone except Henson and four Eskimos: Ootah, Egingwah, Seegloo, and Ooqueah."

Tramaine's brother gave a whistle. "Say those names again. Slow now."

Alvin said them slow, and the other boys repeated after him. And everyone laughed. It was as though they were best friends.

"Ootah saved Henson from freezing to death in icy water once," said Alvin. "And Henson saved Peary from both freezing and starvation."

"Peary was white, right?" said Tramaine's brother. "See how they couldn't do without the brother?"

After they left, Shastri said, "You learned a lot about Henson fast."

"I read a great book," said Alvin. "And I've read others about him before."

"Sounds almost as though you knew him. You got those guys laughing."

"Yeah."

"Watch out," said Shastri.

"What's that mean?"

"Just watch out. Want to ride my bike?"

So they went to Shastri's and took turns riding.

On Wednesday Tramaine sat down by Alvin and Shastri in the lunchroom. Alvin was describing Henson's memorial at Arlington National Cemetery.

"How tall is it?" asked Tramaine.

"I don't know," said Alvin.

"What do you mean, you don't know?" Tramaine said, emphasizing each word. "When you stand by it, how high up does it come on you?"

"I only saw pictures in a book," said Alvin.

"What? The way you love that guy, and you ain't even been to the cemetery? Tell you what—we can go together. The group of us. Today, after school."

Arlington National Cemetery was an easy Metro ride from the stop on the Connecticut Avenue side of the National Zoo. But Mamma didn't allow Alvin to go into white neighborhoods without her. He didn't want to tell Tramaine that, though. The way Tramaine was talking, it was clear his mother didn't put restrictions like that on him.

No one's mother was as strict as Alvin's. "Okay. Sure."

Shastri looked at Alvin funny, but he didn't say anything.

After Tramaine left, Alvin said, "Want to come?"

"With those guys?" said Shastri. "No way. They got trouble written all over them."

"No, they don't," said Alvin.

"What do you think they're doing with you anyway?" asked Shastri.

"Being nice."

Shastri looked disgusted. "They're playing games, that's what. And they're not your type of games."

For the rest of the day, Alvin felt kind of sick inside. Tramaine wasn't really trouble. He did dumb things in school sometimes, like talking back to the teacher, but nothing really bad. It was Tramaine's brother that worried Alvin. People said he worked for the neighborhood drug dealers.

But the guys didn't turn out to be trouble at all. It was fun being with them. They joked the whole time on the Metro. They were laughing as they got out at the cemetery stop and went into the main entrance. Alvin picked up a map of the cemetery at the information booth. But Matthew Henson's memorial wasn't listed. "Excuse me," he said to the woman behind the booth. "Can you tell me where Matthew Henson's buried?"

"The king," said Tramaine's brother Roderick, leaning between them. "Where's his grave?"

"Section eight, grave five-fifteen. Here, let me mark it for you." The woman drew on the map.

Huge, bare oaks and maples lined the path. White headstones—all the same size, the same shape—lined up in horizontal rows, and if you looked across the rows, you could see that they formed diagonal lines, too. It gave the eerie sensation that the cemetery went on forever.

Finally they got to section eight. Alvin stopped and looked around slowly. There it was, a little farther up on the left. He recognized the black granite headstone immediately from the photo in the book. It was big. Majestic.

He knew the whole history of the memorial. Originally Henson had been buried somewhere else, but the government reburied him in Arlington in 1988, because everyone was ashamed that Matthew Henson hadn't received the fame he should have had while he was alive. Robert Peary, the white man, got all the credit. No one had cared about what a black man had done. And no one cared about those four Eskimos, either.

Alvin ran his hand over the bronze insets. The top one was of Henson's head, surrounded by the fur of his Arctic parka. The middle one was Henson flanked by two Eskimos on each side, with the American flag behind, claiming the North Pole. The bottom one was a scene of a dog pack and people in the icy north.

Tramaine and Roderick and their friend Karimu acted properly impressed.

"Look at the dogs," said Tramaine. "'Specially that one." He pointed. "I never saw such a evil face."

"Henson learned to drive them," said Alvin.

Karimu walked to the other side of the memorial. "Come on around here," he called. "Get this." He read out the words chiseled there, "'Codiscoverer of the North Pole.'"

Alvin made a *humph*.

"What's the matter, Dwarf?" said Tramaine.

Alvin walked over to the bigger cement globe behind Henson's memorial. He knew from his book that it was the memorial to Robert Peary, the white man who led the expedition. And he already knew the words that were chiseled on it. He read them aloud now, pointing. "'Discoverer of North Pole.'" He looked at the other guys. "No 'codiscoverer.' Just 'discoverer.'"

"Same old story," said Roderick. "That's the guy who Henson saved, right, Dwarf?"

"Yeah," said Alvin. "But Henson's memorial is better anyway."

"You got that one right, bro," said Karimu.

They walked back to Henson's memorial and stood there, silent. Alvin read the inscription:

THE LURE OF THE ARCTIC IS TUGGING AT MY HEART. TO ME THE TRAIL IS CALLING! THE OLD TRAIL—THE TRAIL THAT IS ALWAYS NEW.

Still no one talked. Then they took the Metro home.

There was something really nice about standing silent together. And there was something really nice about going home without saying another word. No, those guys weren't trouble at all, that's what Alvin thought. That's what he thought on Wednesday night.

But on Thursday things changed. Shastri had to go shopping with his mother, so Alvin walked home from school alone, rolling around those four great names in his mouth—Ootah, Egingwah, Seegloo, and Ooqueah—when he heard snapping fingers. He made the mistake of looking up.

"Hey, my man, you need money?" The guy was skinny and tall. And young—still a teen. But he had that unmistakable drug dealer's look on his face.

"No, thanks." Alvin's mind cleared instantly. This guy was doing business. Business, and in full daylight. He walked faster.

"Hey, you stop when I'm talking to you."

Alvin stopped. His mouth went dry.

"That's better. You the one they call Dwarf, right?" He squinted. "They said you'd do fine—and they were right. Man, you look like you're eight or nine. A foot shorter than Tramaine. You all right."

A group of teenagers walked out of the bakery across the other side of the grassy triangle. They headed this way, and Alvin was pretty sure one of them was the big brother of Tiffany, a girl down the block. But they weren't moving fast enough to make this dealer go.

Alvin stood perfectly still. He wasn't afraid; he was suspended—as though real life had stopped for a moment.

"Come on, you scared? Hell, Santy Claus didn't give you everything you wanted for Christmas now, did he? Maybe he didn't come at all. I hear you ain't got much. No daddy, right?" The dealer ran his tongue between his top teeth and his lip. "You do me a favor and I pay you. Whoa, I'm the one's doing the favor, giving you money, so's you don't have to fight it out with no Santy Claus." The guy jerked his neck as though to get rid of a kink. "I saw you talking to yourself. Pretending, right? With money in your pocket you can forget pretend. You can do. Like a real man." He walked toward Alvin.

Alvin turned and ran.

"What's the matter with you?" called the guy. "You saying no to easy money? Fool. You'll change your mind. Tomorrow, yeah, see you tomorrow."

Alvin ran all the way to the library. He wouldn't chance going home and letting the dealer see where he lived. But how stupid could he get? This dealer knew Tramaine. He could find out where Alvin lived anytime he wanted. Alvin sat down at a table in the main reading room and watched the front door and waited for his heartbeat to slow to normal.

No one came through the library door except a mother and a little kid.

After a while, Alvin went to a window that looked out on 16th Street. He approached it cautiously, from the side, and peeked out quickly. No dealer in sight.

The guy could have been hiding somewhere. Waiting.

Alvin was trapped in the library.

He peeked out the window again. The sidewalk was empty.

This was stupid. He'd go crazy if he kept looking out the window. Grandma wouldn't worry about where Alvin was for at least another couple of hours. So there was no rush. He could outwait the guy. And he should work in the meantime—keep his mind busy.

He found a book on Henson and asked Mrs. Sullivan to print out a copy of the inscription on Henson's memorial. The one he had read over and over inside his head when he'd stood in front of it with Tramaine and Roderick and Karimu. Then he picked out books on the Arctic.

Every once in a while he'd read something he really liked. Like the fact that the great area of land at the southern edge of the Arctic Circle is called the tundra and it's usually frozen but when it thaws in spring, the willow trees color the whole tundra a pale greeny yellow that seems to wave when the wind blows. The trees are ground-creeping plants, less than a foot high. Dwarfs—maybe that's why Alvin liked them so much.

Alvin took notes in his math notebook. He felt guilty using up those pages, but he didn't have anything else. After a long while, he went to one of the front windows—standing this time—and peeked outside. No dealer. He walked home fast.

That night he lay in bed and looked through the dark at the ceiling he couldn't see. The dealer had talked about tomorrow.

On Friday morning Alvin practically ran to Shastri's house. He kept his eyes on the sidewalk the whole way. And when Shastri came out, he just about pulled him the rest of the way to school. It didn't make sense—dealers were hardly ever seen that early in the morning. But he wasn't taking chances.

Later Tramaine came up beside him in the lunch line. "Why'd you run from Duane?"

Duane. The dealer had a normal name, just like anyone else. Alvin shrugged. "I don't know."

"It's easy, man. And for you, it would be even easier."

Alvin scratched his cheek. He didn't want the guys

in front and behind him in line to hear this.

"A dwarf like you, who'd suspect? Not a soul would stop you. You'd be a perfect runner."

Alvin shook his head.

"The money's good."

"I'm not interested," Alvin mumbled.

"Not interested," mimicked Tramaine, but he made Alvin sound prissy when he did it. He shook his head. "I do you a favor—I told Duane about you— and you go back to being white boy. That what your mammy wants?" He walked off.

Alvin tried not to think about Tramaine or Duane or any of those guys all weekend. He read. And he memorized the inscription on Henson's memorial. And he dreamed about unbelievable expanses of white snow under a dazzling sun.

CHAPTER FIVE

Trains

Back in school on Monday, when it was free reading time, Alvin asked permission to use a computer in the resource room. He planned to look up Laila Henson again and this time find her address. He had to write to her soon if he was going to get an answer in time for his project. But instead of typing in her name right off, he started with a map of North America. He just wanted to get a sense of the distance, that's all. He consulted the map key. It was thousands of miles from Washington, D.C., to the North Pole. He clicked a link that led him to a map of northern Canada. He looked past gigantic

Hudson Bay up to the cluster of islands—Baffin Island, the Queen Elizabeth Islands, and then Ellesmere Island. He recognized that last name; that's where Fort Conger was—the base for Matthew Henson's final expedition. The very idea of pitching camp on Ellesmere Island, rather than Greenland, was Henson's. And that decision was probably what made the whole thing succeed.

Parts of Alaska, Canada, Greenland, Scandinavia, and Russia extended into the Arctic Circle. Otherwise, there was ocean, nothing but ocean, all the way to the top of the map.

How could someone get to Fort Conger? Wouldn't that be the ultimate in primary research? Ms. Artiga would be astounded and Alvin would win the prize, that's for sure. He almost laughed out loud. It was impossible, of course. But it didn't hurt to daydream a little.

Alvin went to Google and typed in Fort Conger and Ellesmere Island. Finally he found a good website. There were two research bases on Ellesmere Island: Alert and Eureka. Neither allowed visitors.

Who wanted to go to a research base anyway? Fort Conger was the interesting place. Alvin read that planes could land at Grise Fiord, way up north. But not commercial planes. Small planes that carried six or eight passengers. The price wasn't listed. Instead the website gave the names and phone numbers of trappers you could negotiate a price with from whatever city you wanted.

When a price wasn't listed, it was high, anyone knew that. So that meant someone heading north should first travel as far as possible by train.

Alvin typed in Amtrak.com and found the pages with train schedules. They led him to the Canadian passenger rail services website. He punched the keys fast.

The path was clear. Washington, D.C., to New York. New York to Toronto. Toronto to Winnipeg. Winnipeg to Churchill. That was the end of the line; Churchill was the farthest north any train in Canada went.

Alvin clicked the link to Churchill. Colorful houses lining each side of a narrow street filled the top half of the screen. Underneath was tourist information. Churchill boasted of being located on Hudson Bay. And it had a great museum. And grain elevators.

What kind of a place had grain elevators as its big tourist attraction?

Alvin clicked back to the map. Churchill was far from Grise Fiord. If someone was smart and lucky, maybe he could hitchhike from Churchill north and then call a trapper for a plane the rest of the way. Where did the roads out of Churchill lead?

The blue line that stopped at Churchill—the train line—was the only colored line that touched Churchill. Oh, there were red lines on the map, too. But none of them ran to Churchill. He checked the map key again. As he feared, those red lines were roads. And Churchill had no red lines.

How could a town have no roads in or out of it?

He clicked on various other towns in Canada and on trains leading to them.

Chanelle came into the resource room. "What's up?" She sat at the computer beside Alvin and glanced at his screen. "Ooo, nasty-looking dogs. I'd hate to meet up with one of them. What you doing here anyway?"

"I could ask you the same thing," said Alvin.

"I bet I know what you're doing. Yeah, I know. You working on the social studies project, aren't you? I bet you been reading every night since Ms. Artiga gave the assignment."

"I bet you have, too."

Chanelle smiled. "Everyone wants a prize."

"Yeah. But I'm not working on the project now."

Chanelle slapped him lightly on the shoulder. "So what you doing looking at them ugly dogs, anyway?"

"I wasn't looking at dogs. I was looking at trains." Alvin clicked back to the map of northern Canada.

"Trains in Canada? Like the Polar Express in that kids' book?"

Alvin shrugged.

"Go on," said Chanelle. "Type Polar Express."

"Okay." Alvin tried various combinations again. "Look at this. There's a train into Moosonee. You go from Toronto to Corcoran and hop on it. And guess its name."

"The Polar Express."

"Close. The Polar Bear Express. I want to take it."

"In your dreams." Chanelle laughed. "You'd never have the guts to get near a polar bear in real life. And you'd never travel that far. You the mamma's boy, I hear."

"No, I'm not," said Alvin quickly.

"Chill," said Chanelle, looking over her shoulder. "If you talk too loud, we'll get kicked out," she whispered. "I didn't mean nothing by it. Sorry."

"Anyway, it doesn't take guts to travel. It just takes money," said Alvin. "I've got plenty of money."

"Sure," said Chanelle. "Like I really believe you."

But Alvin did have money.

CHAPTER SIX

Fights

"Alvin?" called Grandma.

"Hi, Grandma." Alvin threw his backpack into the corner. Instantly he felt guilty. Mamma would cry out if she saw him treating his Christmas present like that. He pulled off his jacket and carefully hung it on a hook.

"Come light the pilot on this oven for me."

He went into the kitchen, struck a match, got on his knees, and lit the pilot in the back of the bottom of the oven. Then he sank onto his heels and looked at Grandma. She worked at the kitchen table with a bowl of green beans soaking in water, cutting off the stems and piling them on the board in front of her. Her movements were regular, but slow.

"Green beans. Plain food is good for the soul," said Grandma. "It makes you grateful for holiday food when it comes round again. Now turn that oven to three-fifty, would you? The yams are already on the rack."

Alvin turned the temperature dial. He stood and looked at the bowl of beans. He liked beans. But he'd loved the peanut soup and steamed fish at the Kwanzaa feast. They didn't have enough feasts in this house. "How old were you, Grandma, when you learned about the world?"

Grandma looked surprised. "What you mean, learned about the world?"

"You know. The bad things."

"Something happen to you today?" Grandma put the knife on the board, dried her hands on the dish towel, and pushed herself sideways in her chair so that her lap was exposed. "Come sit here and tell me."

"Grandma, I'm twelve. I don't sit on laps."

"Everyone needs a lap now and then." But she moved her knees back under the table, one at a time. "What happened?"

Alvin ran his hand along the top of the chair that

was opposite Grandma. He felt tears coming. He blinked hard. "I can't remember so many things, Grandma. Important things."

Grandma laughed. "You complaining to me about memory? Lord, boy, don't I know it." She shook her head. "What you want to remember, Alvin?"

"I don't know." Alvin's throat hurt, as though he was trying to swallow something big. "I don't even remember when I learned that Santa Claus wasn't real."

"Who says Santa ain't real?" Grandma's voice was feisty.

"Come on, don't joke." Alvin turned the chair around and sat, straddling it. "I can't remember it. Maybe I always knew."

"I hate that kind of talk." Grandma took a handful of beans from the bowl and put them on the board. She picked up the knife and trimmed those beans with fingers that were suddenly quick and sure. "Santa Claus is an idea, Alvin. If you're so grown-up, you know that. It's up to you whether you let go or hold on for life."

Not much is up to me, thought Alvin. He let his chin drop onto the top of the chair back.

"What's bothering you? Is it that bike—all the time, that bike?"

Alvin blinked back tears again.

Grandma stopped cutting beans and shook her finger at Alvin. "Life's not just about getting things."

"I know that, Grandma. Don't treat me like a little kid."

"You're acting like a little kid." Grandma picked up the cutting board and pushed the pile of beans off into the pot sitting on the table.

"What's the farthest you've ever gone, Grandma?"

"What? Gone? Gone where?"

"That's what I'm asking. Have you ever gone anywhere, Grandma?"

"I used to work in a embassy kitchen when I was young. Down on Massachusetts Avenue. You know that, Alvin."

He got up and headed for the door.

"Alvin."

He stopped in the doorway. "Yes, Grandma?"

"If you let go of Santa Claus, you got no one to blame but Alvin."

Alvin went to the bedroom he shared with Grandma and threw himself backward onto the bed with his shoes on. Then he relented, took his shoes off, and slid them under it. He lay back again.

The next thing he knew, Mamma was calling him

to the table. He must have slept for at least an hour. He went downstairs and tried to act alert. But all through dinner Alvin's mind wandered. His eyes passed from the yams to the beans, to the jug of water, back to the yams. The sweet smell of Mamma's perfume floated heavy in the air. He grunted responses to the questions of the dinner conversation. Before he knew it, they were cleaning up and he was drying the dishes and putting them away.

Grandma went upstairs to their bedroom. He heard her shut the door.

Mamma stood by her shelves near the window, the ones where she kept her bird nests. She picked up the robin nest that Alvin had found for her last spring, on the outside windowsill of an abandoned building. Tips of grasses had sprung loose along one side. Mamma gently tucked them into place. She set the nest back on the sill and washed her hands. "Alvin . . . " She kept her back to him. Then she heaved a sigh and sank onto a chair. "Alvin, how are you, honey? I mean, really?"

"I'm okay." He hung the dish towel on the little rack on the oven door.

"Really?"

No, not really. "Jasmine went to Disney World over the holiday. And Shastri is going to New York next weekend. Even Sabrina goes back to Puerto Rico every year, and her family is poor as dirt."

"What are you talking about, Alvin?"

"I'm going to buy that mountain bike, Mamma. I've got the money and I'm going to buy it."

"We've been through this, Alvin."

"I'm going to see things. I've got to see things."

"You'll see things. When you're old enough to know how to handle them."

"I need a bike now."

"You're thinking about Uncle Pete, aren't you? Don't count on that man, Alvin."

That wasn't a fair thing for Mamma to say. She was always putting Uncle Pete down, calling him unreliable. But that wasn't the point. "I need a bike for myself. So I can go where I want."

"You're not going anywhere, Alvin."

"I'll go all around the world if I want. And you can't stop me."

"You can't have a bike."

"It's fun riding a bike," said Alvin.

She sighed. "What do you know? You can't even ride a bike, Alvin."

"Uncle Pete taught me. And I've ridden friends' bikes."

Mamma looked up sharply.

"I ride fast." His voice rose. "I'm good at it."

Mamma shook her head with her mouth open. Then she gave a little snort. "A bike that costs that much would get stolen in less than a week."

"I'll lock it up."

"What's a lock against chain clippers? For all how smart you are, Alvin, you're not streetwise. I don't want to hear any more about it."

"Shastri keeps his bike inside. I will too."

Mamma gestured toward the chair beside her. "Come on over here. We need to talk."

He didn't move. "I have a right to the bike. I earned the money."

"Hush now, Alvin. We've got to talk. It's about your grandma."

Oh. "I'm sorry I upset her today."

"Did you upset her?" Mamma put her elbow on the table and rested her chin and cheek in the cup of her hand. "You're acting up, Alvin—all this talking back." She shook her head. "But underneath, you're still my good boy. My sweet boy." Her voice caught, as though she was about to cry.

Alvin came over and stood close. "What's the matter?"

"I had to leave work today for a little while. I got paged."

Mamma walked outside all day long, without a cell phone. So if anyone wanted her, they had to call the Park Service and have her paged. Then Mamma would call back as soon as she could get to a phone.

"Who paged you?"

"Mrs. Keys." Mamma sighed. "She paged me last week, too. Grandma fell down—last week and then again this morning."

Mrs. Keys lived upstairs with her son Franklin till he moved out a few months back. She was friends with Grandma, even though she was a lot younger.

Alvin thought of Grandma sitting in the dark on the couch in the morning lately. He should have known something was wrong. "Is Grandma sick?"

"She's just old, Alvin. She can't be alone all day long anymore."

He dropped into the chair beside Mamma. "So what are we going to do?"

"I'm going to pay Mrs. Keys to spend the day with her."

"How much will that cost?"

"Enough." Mamma sighed. "But I'm lucky. Last weekend I applied for a night job at the zoo, cleaning up the grounds after hours. They said I could start next Monday."

"You're going to work at night?"

"Just till nine."

He swallowed. Mamma came home exhausted already. She'd never make it till nine.

Money. They needed money—and Alvin had money. It was unfair, too, too unfair. But what else could he do? "You can have my money. That'll pay for Mrs. Keys till school's out in June, and then I can get jobs again and make enough so you don't have to work nights."

Mamma smiled sadly. "See what a sweetie you are? You keep your money, Alvin. I don't want you supporting a family until you're the man of a family."

"I'm growing up, Mamma."

"Not that fast. Anyway, your money wouldn't last all the way till June."

Really? He'd worked so long for that money—all summer and fall. He felt stupid. He hated money. That's where the Eskimos had everyone beat—they didn't use money. They simply worked and traded for whatever they needed. He took Mamma's free hand.

"I'll make dinner, then. Grandma loves it when I make frozen pizza. And macaroni and cheese. Cooking's easy."

"Don't talk nonsense. Grandma's not about to stop doing everything all at once. Mrs. Keeys is going to help. She'll stick around and eat dinner with you and Grandma. She won't leave till I get home."

"You don't have to pay for all those hours, Mamma. I can take care of Grandma once I get home from school."

"You need taking care of as much as Grandma does."

"That's not true. I look after myself. I did fine with the drug dealer last week."

Mamma's face went slack. "What drug dealer?"

Alvin wished he could take back his words. "It was nothing."

"Tell me, Alvin."

"A guy stopped me and I listened for a moment and then went on."

"You listened!"

"It was nothing, Mamma. I stay out of trouble."

"You listened! And after that article in the news-paper last month—all about strangers preying on kids exactly your age. We talked about it, Alvin. And then you go and listen to one of them! How could you?"

"He wasn't a stranger. He was a friend of Tramaine's big brother."

"Tramaine? You've been talking about this Tramaine a lot lately. You've gone and gotten mixed up with the wrong crowd." Mamma smacked him on the side of the head.

"Ow!"

Her face looked as shocked as Alvin felt. He couldn't remember Mamma ever having hit him before. His gentle mamma. Her eyes filled with tears. She dropped her hand to the table.

Then she sat up tall, resolve hardening her face. "I'm going to ask Mrs. Keeys to walk you to school and back, like Grandma used to do."

"No! You can't do that." It was bad enough that he wasn't allowed to do things everyone else had been doing for years. But this was horrible. And it was happening at just the wrong time—just when Tramaine was saying bad things about him. "Everyone will make fun of me. They used to make fun of me for Grandma and that was back in second grade. I'm way too old, Mamma."

"You're not old enough, not if you're making friends with drug dealers."

"I'm not friends with him—I never saw him before."

"Just a minute ago you said he wasn't a stranger. Are you lying now, Alvin?"

"No, I swear."

"Then why'd you stop to talk to him?"

"I didn't stop to talk to him, Mamma. He stopped me. He tried to talk to me, but I wouldn't talk to him."

"But you listened. All the brains you've got, and look how you act."

"That's not how it was." Alvin jumped to his feet. "You know me better than that. I'll never have anything to do with drugs."

"You bet you won't. I love you too much to let that happen. I can't help having to work all the time—but I'm still doing right as your mother. I'll call Mrs. Keeys tonight." Mamma stood up too. She hugged him. "We have a good home. So you be good. You stay safe. I need you safe. You hear?"

Alvin held himself stiff, unyielding.

"And I want you to give me that money you saved, so you don't go do something foolish with it."

He pulled himself away from her. "What you think, I'm going to spend it on drugs or something?"

"I didn't say that."

He stared at the row of bird nests on the window. He felt like knocking them all off with one swipe. Trashing them. "It's my money."

"I'm raising you decent." Mamma blinked. "We'll go to the bank together on Saturday morning and deposit that money in your college fund. You're going to go to college, Alvin. You're going to be the first one in the family to go." She pushed her hair back with both hands in a gesture of exhaustion. "Grandma needs me to help with her bath."

Alvin was breathing funny. He felt like he was filling up with air and he'd float away. "Tell me something, Mamma."

"What?"

"My class is going to Philadelphia in May. Can I go?"

"Let's not talk about that now. That's months away."

"I might get chosen to help plan the trip. If I help plan it, can I go? Can I go, Mamma?"

Mamma pressed her hand to her mouth. "You're just trying to make us fight more."

"So that's your answer? No. Right?"

"Kids your age need watching, Alvin. That's exactly what you've just proved. The next few years you're going to need the most watching. You belong home." She left.

She didn't trust him. Mamma didn't trust Alvin, when Alvin was the most trustworthy of any of the kids he knew.

Tomorrow Mrs. Keeys would walk him to school. And in May his class would climb on a bus without him.

His whole life long, she'd spoiled things for him. She had no right.

She thought she knew everything. She took it for granted that Alvin would stay at the kitchen table and do his homework, like always.

And tomorrow she expected him to walk to school with Mrs. Keeys by his side. In five minutes of arguing, she had decided to ruin his life. Here he'd been hoping for a new nickname, something better than Dwarf, and now he'd get it all right—Baby, or maybe White Boy Baby, or who knew what horrible thing Tramaine would come up with. Mamma would completely destroy his life—his lousy life that was already falling apart and that had never ever ever been exciting. It was so far from Matthew Henson's life. Oh, Henson didn't have a perfect life. But he never let anything or anyone hold him back. He did things. He went places.

Matthew Alexander Henson was born in 1866. His mother died when he was little, even littler than Alvin was when his father died. Then Henson's father died, too. His stepmother beat him. So he ran away. In the middle of winter—just like now. He cut up his blanket and tied the pieces around his feet to keep them from freezing and he walked from their farm in Maryland all the way to the big city of D.C. He worked in a restaurant—and slept in the kitchen. One of the customers told him about how great it was to be a sailor. So Henson walked to Baltimore and got a job on a ship. By that time he was twelve. Alvin's age.

The captain taught Henson to read. They sailed all around the world. When the captain died, Henson went back to Baltimore and tried another ship. But the captain on that ship was drunk and mean. Then Henson worked in a clothing store and he met Robert Peary and after that he was an explorer, the best explorer. The best in the whole world.

Matthew Henson did all that, and here Alvin was going to be walked to school—walked to school!—at the age of twelve. Mamma thought that would help him. Mamma was so wrong.

And she was wrong about something else, too: Alvin wasn't going to sit here and do his homework.

He went into the living room and turned off the light. That way he could see out. He stood at the window, raised the shade, and peered into the night. The bottom tip of the triangle of grass in the middle of Mount Pleasant Street was just visible from here. Two men, heads together, hands in their pockets, huddled against the wind. The sidewalk up and down Lamont Street was empty. Someone leaned on an overturned trash can in the side alley across the street. Alvin could see the bottle in his hand. So that made three people out on the street at eight thirty. All of them just waiting for something to happen.

Maybe those three people spent their whole lives just waiting for something to happen. Maybe they had never gone outside Washington, D.C. Maybe not even as far as Massachusetts Avenue, where Grandma worked when she was young.

Alvin stood in the dark, seething. The worst part, the very worst, was that Mamma knew what he was missing, because his father had taken her traveling. His father had a wanderlust—that's what Uncle Pete used to say. He'd go traveling with anyone anywhere at the drop of a hat. Mamma had even been to San Francisco, clear across the country.

But Mamma said Alvin wasn't going anywhere. He belonged home.

Oh, he understood she wanted only to protect him—but that didn't make it any easier to take.

No bike trip with Uncle Pete. No class trip in May. Nowhere ever. Just here. Forever and ever and ever.

With everyone laughing at him, even the nice kids who didn't know a thing about Tramaine. They'd see Mrs. Keeys and fall down laughing.

Alvin was dying under Mamma's protection. Sometimes he felt already dead.

CHAPTER SEVEN

Getting Ready

Alvin opened the basement door. The light for the steps didn't work. He got the flashlight from under the kitchen sink and went downstairs. His old sleeping bag lay on top of the folded-up tent. No one had used the camping equipment since Uncle Pete moved to Philadelphia. He picked up the mess kit and fingered the best pocketknife in the world. It had two blades and it had belonged to his father when he was a boy, that's what Uncle Pete had said. Alvin opened the blades and felt the edges. They were as sharp as ever. He slipped the knife into his pocket and picked up the sleeping bag.

Upstairs Alvin poured vegetable oil on a paper

towel. Then he opened the knife and rubbed both blades with it. That's what Uncle Pete used to do.

He spread the sleeping bag on the hall floor. It smelled like the basement. He climbed the stairs quietly and listened at the bathroom door. It was empty. He took Grandma's baby powder from the top of the back of the toilet. She always said nothing smelled better than a baby's bottom as she patted it under her arms. He sprinkled the inside of the sleeping bag. Now it smelled like a musty baby. He rolled it up as tight as he could, tied it firmly, and put it in the corner. He took his jacket off the hook and arranged it over the sleeping bag so that it looked like it had been dropped there. When Mamma came out later to double-check that the doors were locked before she went to bed, she wouldn't see the sleeping bag.

He stuck the knife in his backpack. Then he checked the compass in the side pocket of his pack, where he always carried it, just in case. The little dial swung freely and pointed to the front of the house. His father had given it to him when he was only three years old, and he'd actually kept it safe all this time. He didn't remember his father giving it to him, of course. He didn't remember him teaching Alvin how to use it. But he had. That's what mattered. His father understood what an explorer needed. His father would understand what he was about to do. His father must have loved Matthew Henson, too. Or he would have if he knew about him.

The flashlight was still in his hand. A flashlight could come in handy. But Mamma and Grandma needed it. He put it back under the kitchen sink.

Then he took a one-and-a-quarter-pound bag of Oreos from the cupboard. Neither Mamma nor Grandma really liked Oreos that much. And this way Alvin wouldn't have to buy a meal till he got to New York, at the least. Somehow he'd already decided New York was step number one out of a lot of steps. It was as though the back of his mind was working on the trip while the front of his mind was stuffing his backpack. And now he felt like the back of his mind had led him to check out the Canadian train schedules this morning. A sense of inevitability cloaked him.

He looked through the cupboard one more time. Nothing else seemed essential. Hmmm, maybe a can of tuna. In case of a protein emergency. His pocketknife could open that can.

Next he put in the printout of the inscription on Henson's memorial. That way, he couldn't forget those great words. On second thought, he got worried the paper might get crushed. So he took it out, slid it carefully inside the cover of his spare notebook, and put the notebook into his pack. That worked good.

The hardest part would be putting clothes into his backpack without Grandma knowing. Alvin went into the bedroom with his half-empty pack in his hand. He was lucky: Grandma had gone into the bathroom. He took his black sweatpants with the pockets, a blue sweatshirt, three pairs of socks, and three pairs of underwear. The pack zipped shut with difficulty. He shoved it under his bed. Then he pulled it out again and ran to his top drawer. He took out his money and checked to see that it was all there.

"You counting your money, Alvin?" Grandma walked to her bed without waiting for an answer. "Counting don't make it grow." She laughed. Usually Grandma's laugh was something he loved. Usually it made him laugh, too. But his head hurt too much to laugh now. His head throbbed.

Alvin waited till Grandma began her routine of plumping her pillow, then rolling around to find the right position. While she was grunting, he opened his backpack, pulled out a pair of socks, stuffed the money into a sock, and jammed everything back in again. Then he zipped it all up and shoved it under the bed once more. Grandma didn't say a thing.

The night passed slowly. Alvin watched the shadows formed by the streetlights. He listened to Grandma's snores. It was hours before he slept.

The next morning he dressed in long underwear and jeans, two pairs of socks, and two sweatshirts. Even with his jacket, that wouldn't be enough to keep him warm in the Arctic. But it would probably do for a long way. And he'd face the need for warmer clothes later, if he really did get that far.

When he went out the apartment door, Mrs. Keeys was already in the hallway, waiting to walk him to school. He thought he'd die. The only thing that kept him alive was the knowledge that this would be the one and only time she'd do it, because he'd be gone in a few hours at most.

Mrs. Keeys nodded at him. "Morning, Alvin."

"Morning."

She glanced at his sleeping bag. But she didn't say anything. She was nice that way. In fact, she was really nice.

"Please, Mrs. Keeys." Alvin raised his eyes to her plaintively. "If you walk with me, everyone will call me a baby."

Mrs. Keeys looked at Alvin with bleary eyes. Her

cataracts must be coming back. Mamma said she was unlucky to have them so young. "I know. But your mother asked me to."

"Then walk a block behind me. If I have a problem, you can be there in a minute."

"I don't know, Alvin. I don't see so good."

"I'll wave my arms over my head if I need you. And that's not going to happen anyway. No one messes with kids on their way to school. Please."

Mrs. Keeys fingered the buckle on her jacket belt. Her mouth moved in little puckers. Finally she threw her shoulders back. "You're right. Alice has gone too far this time. I told her, I said, 'Your boy's almost an adolescent.' I said, 'It's a mistake, Alice.'" Mrs. Keeys pointed ahead. "You go on now, Alvin. One block ahead."

So that's how they did it.

When Shastri yelled from his front stoop, "Hey, Dwarf, wait up. What's going on?" Alvin just walked faster. He walked past Chanelle with a bunch of girls and past Chuck, all alone. He didn't say anything to anyone. But he knew he hadn't fooled anyone, either.

When everyone else went to morning recess, Alvin snuck back to the resource room to check out the train schedules again. And, just for good measure, he did another search about the Arctic. The screen filled with information about a book: *The North Pole* by Robert E. Peary. The words at the bottom of the screen made his heart hurt. The original edition of the book had been sold to the people who ran the website by a man named Mark Seltzer.

Mark Seltzer and his wife had died when their kayak flipped in fifteen-foot waves off Baffin Island.

Alvin decided he had read enough. He picked up his sleeping bag from his locker and walked out of school.

CHAPTER EIGHT

Union Station

The triangle of grass in the middle of Mount Pleasant Street marked the end of the bus line. That meant that the bus sat there empty between dropping off passengers from its last round, circling the triangle, and taking on passengers for its next round.

Alvin stood across the street from the bus stop and pressed his back against the front window of the bakery. He didn't see any of his mother's friends about, but he kept his scarf tied around his head so that it covered his nose anyway, just in case. A line of people got on the bus. Once everyone was on, the bus would sit there until five minutes to the hour. It always stuck to schedule.

Alvin was going to wait till the last minute to get on, in case anyone who knew Mamma got on first. His forehead and back were damp. The air was cold, but he was sweating from the combination of all those layered clothes and a nervousness that made him feel almost sick to his stomach. His eyes hurt a little from the bad night's sleep.

Mrs. Ford came out onto her front stoop and looked around. She knew Alvin so well she might recognize him even under his hat and scarf. Alvin pulled his hat down harder and pulled his scarf up higher. For once in his life he was glad Mamma had bought something too big for him, because the hat easily reached to his eyes. He got down on one knee and retied his shoelace. That way Mrs. Ford wouldn't be able to know how tall he was and maybe recognize him by his size. His fingers fumbled with the laces because he still had his gloves on. He could hardly make a bow. Alvin pulled off the gloves and jammed them into his pockets.

When he dared to look up again, Mrs. Ford had gone back inside and the bus was revving up. The doors closed. Alvin dashed across the street in front of the bus and banged on the doors. The driver frowned and opened them. Alvin climbed on. "Thank you."

Alvin paid and stood in the aisle. He shifted his backpack for greater comfort and held the sleeping bag under his left arm. With his right hand he gripped the overhead loop tight. It was high and he had to stretch his arm full length to reach it. His whole body was taut.

He got off at Dupont Circle with almost everyone else and headed for the Metro entrance. Suddenly it was a different world. The little group of people of color from Alvin's bus dissolved in the white flood. Alvin felt conspicuous and small at the same time.

He stood at the top of the escalator and watched it go deep into the black hole. The angle was steep. If he tripped, he'd go flying down. The bulk of his sleeping bag banged against his leg and made him clumsy. This escalator was not a good idea. But before Alvin could turn aside, he was forced onto the top moving step by an old man behind him. He clutched the handrail tight.

He bought a one-way ticket to Union Station. That's where Amtrak trains went into and out of D.C.

The signs in the Metro were easy to follow. Alvin

didn't have to ask a single person for help.

Union Station was huge, with stairs everywhere and food courts and clothing stores and flower vendors. Even though Alvin had been there last June, when he took the train to Uncle Pete's, he still had to wander a long time before he found the ticket lines.

"Please, sir, what's a ticket to Toronto cost?" he asked. Toronto was step number two in his journey. He figured he might as well look ahead.

The ticket salesman typed in his keyboard. "You have to change trains in New York, you know."

"Yes, sir."

"And the next train out of here for New York gets you in too late for the connection to Toronto. So you have to stay in New York overnight."

Alvin felt a muscle twitch in his cheek.

"One-way or round-trip?" asked the man.

"One-way."

He looked past Alvin. "You with anyone?"

"Not right now, sir."

"Children your age can't travel alone without a signed consent from a parent or guardian. And then you have to pay adult fare. Step aside, please," said the man. "Next."

Alvin stepped to one side. That's when he spied

the overhead sign above the information booth, list-
ing all the trains. A train with the endpoint of New
York was supposed to be at platform J. The letter
beside the train's name was flashing. Alvin tapped a
man in a suit on the arm. "Excuse me, sir. Do you
know what the flashing light means?"

"Train's boarding." The man looked at Alvin curiously. "But that train requires reservations. There's
another one in a little less than an hour that anyone
can ride, if you can wait that long." He winked. "It
costs less."

Alvin gave a little smile of gratitude. He walked
over to the benches where lots of people were waiting and sat down. There were several lines at the
ticket counter. He could try a different salesman,
if only he could find a way around the need for a
parent.

Alvin studied the people in the waiting room. A
woman with a baby and a toddler sat on the bench
nearest the wall. They were black. Instantly the
answer came to him.

He walked over and sat on the bench opposite the
woman and her children. He took off his backpack
and set it on top of his sleeping bag on the floor. He
dug out his money sock and held it with one hand

under his shirt. Then he went to the ticket counter and got in a new line.

He kept looking back at his stuff. If anyone stole it, at least he had his money.

Finally he was at the head of the line. "Excuse me, sir. My mother wants one more ticket to New York." Alvin had decided ahead of time that asking for New York was easier than asking for Toronto. No one would give him trouble about changing trains or spending the night. "Child's fare. One-way, please."

"Where's your mother?"

Alvin jerked his chin toward the woman, who was now feeding the baby while the toddler ran back and forth on the bench.

"The next train?"

"Yes, sir."

"She should come over here and buy it herself." But even as the ticket salesman said that, he was punching keys. He held out the ticket. "Thirty-two dollars. And be sure to have your mother sign on the line in the upper left corner. That way if she loses it, no one else can use it."

Alvin paid and went to his bench. By now someone at school must have realized he was missing. He felt the need to blend in.

He got up and moved over to the bench where the woman sat. The infant was asleep on her lap now and the toddler was sitting on the floor beating up a stuffed animal.

He sat back and tried to look like he belonged with them.

After a while, the woman got up and took the little girl by the hand. They walked off.

Alvin got up, too. He checked the train sign above the information booth. A train with the endpoint of New York was flashing. Platform J again.

The signs to the platforms were easy to follow. Everyone at waiting area J lined up. A woman in uniform looked at tickets as the line filed past her through a door. Alvin studied the passengers—mostly white folk in business clothes. One black man had two boys with him. Alvin cut in line behind him.

When they were almost to the door, Alvin got out of line. He looked around desperately, then he ran to the back of the line.

When Alvin got up to the ticket lady, he held up his ticket and willed himself to stay calm.

"You alone?"

"My dad and brothers." Alvin pointed toward the door beyond her.

The woman seemed doubtful for a moment. Then a look of recognition came into her eyes. She nodded. "Catch up with them and don't get separated again."

Alvin got onto the nearest train car and slipped into an empty set of two seats. He put his sleeping bag under the seat near the window and sat with his backpack on his lap and his jacket still on. He stayed tensed up, ready. His eyes darted up and down the car. He studied every new person that got on. The seats were pretty much full now.

The train pulled out of the station.

Everything was quiet.

So far, so good.

CHAPTER NINE

Tired

A woman sat down beside Alvin. A white lady. He looked at her. She gave a businesslike blink and opened a briefcase. She took out a laptop computer and stared in concentration.

Alvin leaned back in his seat and enjoyed the feeling of the train accelerating. Nothing bad could happen between here and New York. So he had time to plan things.

What next?

He'd have a cheap meal in New York. A hot dog or something. Alvin opened his backpack and located the bag of Oreos. He pulled out a wrapped stack and stashed it in the side zipper pocket for emergencies.

The woman beside him muttered. He leaned toward her, straining to hear.

She looked at him abruptly. "Am I bothering you?"

"No, ma'am," said Alvin. He sat straight up again. He should have known she wouldn't have been talking to him.

"I have to give a presentation in Philadelphia in three hours," said the woman, still looking at him. Her cheeks were blotchy red, her eyes watery and nervous. "I like to practice right before."

Alvin didn't know how to respond. Now that she really was talking to him it surprised him. He had to say something, just to be polite. "My uncle lives in Philadelphia."

"What does he do?"

"Huh?"

"What does he do for a living?"

"He works for Sun Oil. Or he used to. I'm not sure who he works for now."

"Oh." The woman kept looking at Alvin, waiting for him to say more.

"I guess we've got three hours together," said Alvin.

"Oh, we'll be in Philly in two hours. But I've got

to get from the Thirtieth Street Station over to
Fifteenth and Market. And grab a bite to eat. And
then compose myself." The woman looked at a chart
on her screen. Then she looked back at Alvin. "How
old are you?"

"Twelve."

"Well, then, you must buy a lot of things for yourself."

Alvin thought about that. "What do you mean?"

"You do your own shopping now, right? Not for
clothes, probably. But for toys and things."

Alvin almost shook his head. But he could see that
the woman wanted him to say yes. "Well, sure."

The woman's face brightened. "Do you ever think
about advertising?"

Alvin cleared his throat. He had no idea what she
was talking about. "No, ma'am."

"I think about it all the time." She tapped the
chart with her finger. "It's my job, figuring out how
to get people your age to buy things." She turned her
head and stared at the chart. Her lips moved in
silent speech now.

Alvin's eyelids drooped. He was turning his head
to get more comfortable when he happened to
glance forward. A conductor had walked into their

car. Alvin stood up to see better. The conductor talked to the people in the first row of seats. They showed him their tickets. Alvin sat back down.

The woman watched Alvin. "Are you alone?" she asked abruptly, with a little rise of panic in her voice.

Alvin shook his head. "My dad," he mumbled.

"Oh." The woman looked clearly relieved. "Where is he? Why aren't you sitting with him?"

"My little brothers are with him. There weren't enough seats."

"Oh." She went back to studying her chart.

It was amazing, really, how easy it was to lie. Alvin normally valued honesty. But succeeding in this journey demanded certain lies. And the lies didn't hurt anyone, after all. Still, he promised himself that he wouldn't tell lies unless he really needed to. He yawned, lack of sleep was catching up with him.

Alvin stood up again and peeked over the seat in front of him. The conductor was making his way down the rows of seats.

Alvin looked at his ticket. It was fully paid for. He'd hand it over just like everyone else. The conductor would probably assume Alvin and the woman were together. Everything could work out.

Then he remembered the warning of the ticket

salesman: Someone was supposed to sign the top left corner of the ticket. What happened if it wasn't signed? Alvin hugged his backpack. "Would you . . . " Alvin stopped himself.

"What?" The woman looked at him oddly.

"Nothing."

Alvin stood up again. The conductor was about a fourth of the way down the car.

"Are you all right?" asked the woman.

Alvin nodded yes. He fell back into his seat. Then he shook his head no.

"Do you need to use a bathroom?" she whispered. "There's one at the end of the car."

"Oh, yeah." He could hide in the bathroom.

"I thought so. I don't have children, but I know how you all are. It's my job to think about how children are." She smiled kindly. "Go ahead. I'll watch your things for you."

Alvin looked at the rear end of the car, the end nearest him. There was the bathroom with a little water fountain outside it. "I'm going," he said.

The woman nodded agreeably.

Alvin pushed his backpack under the seat in front of him until it didn't show. Then he made sure his sleeping bag, under his own seat, didn't show. He got out in the aisle. "I might go talk to my dad, too, so I won't be back for a while."

The woman gave a brief smile.

Alvin went straight to the bathroom. It was occupied. He looked back at the conductor. The conductor was talking to a passenger. Alvin pulled a cup out of the dispenser and filled it with water. The train jolted and he spilled a little. He gulped down the rest. A woman came out of the bathroom. Alvin went in. He wished he had a watch. Well, he'd just stay in the bathroom a long time.

He closed the lid of the toilet and sat on top of it. After a long while, he went back to his seat, leaned his head against the window, and shut his eyes. Inside his jacket he was heating up really bad, but the cold glass felt good on his forehead. The train rocked gently.

CHAPTER TEN

Penn Station

"Next stop, Penn Station."

Alvin rubbed his eyes. His mouth felt fuzzy with sleep.

"Penn Station, New York," called the conductor.

New York already? Alvin looked down in a panic. But his stuff was exactly where he'd left it. He slipped on his backpack and held his sleeping bag. The woman beside him had disappeared. Naturally. Maybe she was already giving her presentation in Philadelphia.

The train stopped. People filed off. Down out of the train, then up the escalator.

Alvin hurried through the huge train station—so

many stores, so many people in a hurry, so much noise.

A woman slid a full tray of glazed doughnuts behind a glass counter. The sweet smell caught him. He hesitated for a moment. *Smack*. He staggered. Someone had knocked into his shoulder from behind. The stranger shot him a glance of concern, then went on.

Alvin fought off the sensation of feeling lost. He wasn't lost. He had left, that's all. And he had a goal. And he'd return after a short while. That was different from being lost, way different.

He found a waiting room with two columns that had four phones each on them. The wall clock said 4:52. He went to the phones and dialed.

The line was dead.

He tried another phone.

Dead.

Two broken phones in a row? No way.

Through the glass walls of the waiting room, he could see an older boy leaning against a post. He picked up his stuff and went out toward him. He stopped about fifteen feet away. "Hey."

The boy didn't react.

"Hey, can you help? I have to make a phone call."

The boy looked at him. "You talking to me?"

"I think maybe I'm doing something wrong. Two phones in a row were dead."

"Oh, yeah?" The boy sauntered over. "Where you calling?"

"D.C. Washington, D.C."

"You got money?"

Alvin held out four quarters.

The boy took them. "Lead the way."

Alvin walked into the waiting room.

The boy ran off.

Alvin clutched his sleeping bag hard. A dollar gone—when he needed every penny. He would never have done something that dumb back home. Traveling made him stupid.

Had traveling made that couple stupid—the couple in the kayak that he'd read about this morning?

He leaned against the wall for a moment. He couldn't afford to think about the danger of fifteen-foot waves. He wasn't going to chicken out. This was his chance. And it felt like he'd been waiting for it his whole life.

He knew how to be smart. He wouldn't give money to anyone else. And he wouldn't get in a kayak. Anyway, probably no one got in kayaks in January. So waves didn't matter.

He walked up to a woman. "Excuse me, ma'am. I have to make a call. But I can't seem to get the phones to work."

"How many did you try?"

"Two."

The woman smirked. "Sometimes half the phones in this place are broken. Try another one."

"Thanks." Alvin went to a third phone and dialed. He put in a handful of quarters. It was working. How stupid he'd been to panic like that.

Okay, so here he was on the phone. Grandma should answer in a minute. He'd say he was all right and not to worry and he'd be home pretty soon. She wouldn't be satisfied at that, but it was the best he could do, and she'd be okay. She knew how to let things go.

The phone rang. And rang.

Sometimes Grandma could be slow.

It rang eleven more times. Finally he hung up.

How strange. Grandma had to be home. She should be waiting there, upset that he hadn't come back from school with Mrs. Keeys, sipping tea to calm herself. Maybe she was in the bathroom.

He collected his quarters, struggled out of his backpack, pulled off his jacket, and took a seat.

Someone had left a newspaper on the floor. He picked it up and his eyes strayed sideways through the glass wall. A figure jumped back behind that same post the boy had been leaning against earlier, the boy who took his money. Maybe he was back. Maybe he thought Alvin was an easy mark. Well, as long as Alvin stayed in the waiting room with all these people around, that kid wouldn't bother him. He put the newspaper on the seat beside him and looked straight ahead.

A man and his wife got in a kayak and paddled out to their death. They had wanted to see the Arctic, and they'd died for it. People died for all sorts of things. Little things. Just being in the wrong place at the wrong time.

Alvin rubbed the back of his neck. He went to the phone and dialed again.

No answer.

He walked around the room, keeping his eye on his stuff.

A policewoman came in. Alvin fought the urge to flee. He took his seat and pretended to read the newspaper. He peeked around the edge of the pages. The policewoman strolled through the waiting room. Was she searching for a boy his age—a boy so short his nickname was Dwarf? She stood under the clock and talked into a cell phone.

If she was going to arrest him, she'd have done it by now. Right?

Anyway, he wasn't a criminal. He shouldn't get arrested just for leaving home for a little while. Right?

Alvin watched the clock.

After a long time, the policewoman left.

But he couldn't call now. It was too late; Mamma was home for sure. She'd answer instead of Grandma. And there was nothing he could say to calm Mamma.

Unless he told her he was coming back.

His head got totally quiet. He couldn't hear anything. He thought of a man and woman in a kayak in fifteen-foot waves.

But then he thought of Matthew Henson's eyes on the cover of the school book, always alert, always brave.

On Henson's first expedition to the North Pole, in 1895, the men almost starved because their walrus meat froze too hard to eat. On the second one, their ship got stuck in the ice and Peary lost all but two of his toes to frostbite. They turned black and fell off.

In two more expeditions, everything seemed to go wrong—they ran out of food and had to eat their dogs and almost didn't make it back to base camp. But in 1909 they finally reached the pole. And through all those trials, Henson never wanted to give up. Never.

Henson didn't see the North Pole as desolate. He recognized how beautiful it was because he looked around with eyes that were ready for anything. He saw what the Eskimos saw. He did what they did. He survived that way. He never let traveling make him stupid.

If Alvin stayed alert now, if he looked at things the way Matthew Henson did, he could go anywhere, do anything.

Why, just look, he'd already made it to New York. Here he sat, in Penn Station. He could hardly believe it. He'd never expected to get this far. Not really. He figured he'd be lucky if he made it on a train out of D.C. No one in his class had ever traveled alone this far, he was sure. No one would even dream of trying. But he had done it. And if he could make it this far, he could make it to Ellesmere Island.

All right, then. A phone call was impossible.

Instead he'd send Mamma and Grandma letters. Often. That way they'd be okay. He couldn't bear the idea of them sad.

He turned his head fast and looked right at the post. No one stood there. No one jumped behind it.

He looked down at his clothes. Should he find a bathroom and change? No, he didn't want to dirty his other clothes yet. And anyway, if the police were already looking for him, they would be looking in D.C., not New York. They would still be looking around Mount Pleasant.

He studied the people in the waiting room. None of them seemed likely to help him buy a ticket. And he didn't see any ready-made family that he could pretend to belong to, so he couldn't repeat the trick he'd pulled in Union Station.

Well, that was okay. He had time. The train he wanted didn't leave for Canada till morning.

He put on his jacket and backpack, picked up his sleeping bag, and headed out of the station.

CHAPTER ELEVEN

Cornrows

It was dark, and the streetlights made it hard to see the stars but easy to see the people who marched past on the sidewalks as though they all had something incredibly important to do. Out of nowhere Alvin found he couldn't keep from smiling. This was New York, after all, the Big Apple—that's what Shastri called it. His family went to a Broadway show once every year. He'd be here in just a few days. Wouldn't it be funny if Alvin saw Shastri on the streets of New York? That idea made him smile even more. Shastri always came home from the Big Apple full of descriptions of street vendors who sold spicy sausages and candied almonds you could smell for blocks. But nothing he'd said could have prepared Alvin for this. New York on an ordinary day was more frenetic than Christmas in D.C. Just breathing the cold, noisy air jolted him.

On the other side of the honking traffic was a sandwich shop. He stepped out into the crowd. It washed him along to the corner, as though the people formed a human wave. He crossed with the crowd and went into the shop and took a table by the front window so he could watch everything outside.

A waitress came up. "What'll it be?"

"Could I just sit here?" Alvin looked around. "I mean, as long as the place isn't full? Please?"

The waitress raised her eyebrows. She was large and pink and she smelled like food. "You want to just sit here?"

"Yes, ma'am."

Her eyebrows climbed higher. "You're not hungry?"

He was hungry, very hungry, but he'd had some Oreos for lunch, and that had to be enough till he reached the next step in the trip. He was determined not to spend money before it was absolutely necessary, or he'd run out. And he'd already lost those four quarters to the boy in the station. "No, ma'am," he said.

"Are you a runaway?"

Alvin shook his head.

"What's with the sleeping bag?"

"I'm going camping." What a lame answer. But he couldn't make up a better one on the spot like that.

The waitress walked backward a few steps. Then she turned and hurried toward the kitchen. Before she went through the swinging door, she looked over her shoulder at him.

He imagined her calling the cops. Everything would be over before it had hardly begun. He picked up his stuff and ran. Down to the corner, left, to the next corner, right across the street.

A sign halfway down the block advertised that it was open all night: a coffee shop. He went in and took a table in the rear.

The waiter looked at Alvin as he wiped off the counter. Then he took his time coming to Alvin's table.

"I'm waiting for someone," said Alvin quickly. "I'm not ordering yet."

The waiter nodded and left.

Alvin folded his arms on the table. His cheeks felt heavy and his tongue felt thick. Who would have thought one day of traveling would make him so tired? And it hadn't even been a full day.

The man two tables over slurped soup. The waiter

took an order from a couple who came in and sat at the counter. A woman had left a half-eaten hamburger on a plate near them. Ketchup oozed out the side. It looked wonderful. Alvin got up—but the waiter cleared the burger away.

Deep in his pack was that can of tuna, for an emergency. But if the waiter saw him eating that, he might kick him out. And this wasn't a true emergency anyway. He could always eat more Oreos—but the thought made nausea rise in his throat.

Forget food.

How had he gotten there? He retraced his footsteps in his head. It would be easy to get back to the train station.

He listened again to the man with the soup. The regularity of the slurping mesmerized him. Alvin lay his head on his arms.

"Hey, kid, wake up." A hand shook his shoulder.

Alvin opened his eyes and jerked to attention.

A young woman leaned over him with worry on her face. "It's five thirty. The breakfast crowd is starting. This shift gets busy fast. If you're not eating, you'll have to go."

The breakfast crowd? At five thirty? Alvin looked around. It was still dark outside the plate-glass windows. He sat back and stretched. His neck hurt and his shoulders hurt. He had slept the whole night in his jacket and he was all sweaty.

His stuff!

He jumped up. There was his sleeping bag. He searched through his pack. Everything was there.

He sank into his seat again. His mouth felt dirty. He poured salt from the shaker on the table into his palm. Then he picked up his stuff and went to the bathroom. He dug his toothbrush out of the pack. The hot-water faucet didn't seem to work. He splashed his face and brushed his teeth with salt. That's what Henson used to do when he was on an expedition.

As he stepped out of the bathroom, the girl handed him something rolled up in a napkin. "Don't open it in here or you'll get me in trouble."

There were good people in this world. Thank you, God.

He walked to the end of the block and turned left. Up ahead was the station. He crossed the street and went directly to the waiting room. Buying a ticket could come later; he needed to eat now. The first available seat was beside a teenage girl who wore her hair in cornrows.

Alvin opened the napkin the waitress had given him. A giant bagel rolled off his lap onto the floor. It was stuffed with cream cheese. He picked it up reverently and wiped it with the napkin.

The girl turned to him. "You're not going to eat it now, are you?" She talked funny. And she sat there all straight and prissy.

"The floor's not so bad." He took a big bite. Great bagel.

"That's disgusting. You'll get a disease."

Alvin chewed and swallowed. This girl's shoes were shiny. Her clothes were totally neat. She seemed plastic, except for her hair—it was alive and real. She reminded him of Shastri's cousin, the one who visited on holidays and acted like she was better than everyone. He looked right at the girl, grinned, and took another bite.

"Why do American boys have to act like such pigs?" The girl tapped her fingers on the grip of her suitcase and looked away.

A surge of wickedness filled Alvin. He thrust the bagel in front of the girl's face. "Want a bite?"

The girl smacked Alvin's hand away and the bagel landed on the floor again, but this time it landed with a splat; the two halves had come apart and both lay cream-cheese side down.

He picked up the bagel halves. Pieces of dirt stuck in the cream cheese. Alvin wiped off the floor with his napkin and dropped the whole mess in the trash can by the door.

He went back to his seat and sighed. He was wicked so infrequently, it wasn't fair he had to pay so dearly for it. He turned to the girl beside him. "Look what you did."

The girl lifted her chin. "Shifting the blame. They have names for that in psychology." She opened her big purse and pulled out a tin box. She pried the lid off and took out a cinnamon bun. The rich smell made Alvin dizzy. There had to be more in there. Lots more. The girl took a bite.

"Could I have a bun?" asked Alvin.

The girl acted liked she hadn't heard.

"That bagel was my breakfast," Alvin said.

The girl finished her cinnamon bun.

"My whole breakfast," he said.

The girl looked at him. "I have a long way to travel." She put the box back in her purse. "There's no point in trying to make me feel sorry for you. I won't be manipulated."

"And I didn't have dinner last night," said Alvin.

"What kind of parents do you have, that don't feed you?"

Alvin didn't answer. He felt disloyal for not sticking up for Mamma. Mamma would never let him go to bed hungry. She'd be mortified if she heard what this girl had just said. But if he was going to get any of the food in that tin box, he had to make the girl feel sorry for him. And it was the truth anyway. "I'm hungry."

"I'm going all the way to Canada," the girl said. "I'll be on the train overnight and then most of tomorrow. I need my food."

Alvin's empty stomach knotted. This girl was going to Canada. It was a real place to her, not just a click on a computer screen. "You going to Toronto?"

The girl blinked several times.

He took that as a yes. "You going north of Toronto?"

The girl looked down at her lap.

"You going to Moosonee?" He didn't know why he asked that. He had already decided he was going to Churchill—which was a different direction from Moosonee. Churchill was the right way to go if he wanted to make it to Matthew Henson's outpost at Fort Conger on Ellesmere Island.

But right now he'd asked this girl if she was going to Moosonee, as though the word came out of his mouth on its own. Was he chickening out so soon?

The more he thought about it, though, the more Moosonee seemed like a good idea. "So," said Alvin, "you going? You going to Moosonee?"

The girl tsked. "Is that the way you usually talk?"

"Huh?"

"Speak right or people will think you're stupid. Say 'Are you going to Moosonee?' not 'You going to Moosonee?'" She mimicked him, talking in a super-slow drawl.

"You sound like my mother." Alvin felt a little lump of homesickness. "She always corrects me. She wants people to know I'm smart. But my grandmother says people who want to think you're stupid will do it no matter what. So you might as well talk natural."

"I talk quite naturally." The girl's voice rose as though she'd been insulted.

Alvin was surprised at her reaction. Maybe all her friends ragged on her for talking stiff. Probably this girl was a real outsider. "You talk okay," he said softly. "Only you got a funny accent."

"I'm Canadian. And you're the one with the funny accent."

She certainly wasn't easy to like. He tried again: "Are you going to Moosonee or not?"

"No. I'm going to Winnipeg."

"Have you ever been to Moosonee?"

"No."

"I'm thinking about going there."

The girl knitted her brows. "How?"

"By train." Alvin hesitated. "The Polar Bear Express."

"You can't take a train to Moosonee now," said the girl. "The Polar Bear Express runs only in the summer. It's wilderness over there. There's nothing to see or do except in summer, and then the only thing to visit is a Cree village. If it's polar bear country you want, you have to go north—to Churchill."

Churchill again. He did want to go to Churchill. If he had the guts.

But this girl said Churchill was in polar bear country. Churchill's website hadn't said anything about polar bears. Or not the part Alvin had read anyway. Humongous polar bears. He stood his sleeping bag on end between his feet and squeezed it with his knees. "Have you ever been there?" he asked.

"No. I know about it, though. The train from Winnipeg takes two nights."

Everything in Canada was so far apart. He knew that from the map on the computer, but hearing it was different. He pressed the heels of his hands against his closed eyes.

The girl cleared her throat. "Is everything okay?"

He didn't know if anything was okay.

"What's the matter?" Her voice got very quiet. "You're not really going anywhere, are you?"

"I'm going to Churchill."

"You're only saying that because I mentioned Churchill."

Alvin opened his eyes. "That's not true. I know about Churchill. It has grain elevators. And a museum."

"Oh." The girl pursed her lips thoughtfully. "I guess you'll start out on the Maple Leaf, then. To Toronto. Toronto's the end of the line. You have to change trains to go anyplace else. Then you'll have to take the overnight to Winnipeg, like me." Her tone was nicer now, almost kind. "It's sort of fun. And cheaper than an airplane."

Alvin looked at the girl. She knew how the trains worked. And she had food with her. And she wasn't all that mean, not really. He sort of liked her. "Why you here in the first place?"

"I already told you not to talk like that. If you're going to talk to me, speak properly, please."

Alvin smiled. Boy, was she easy to bug. "You ruined my breakfast. That makes you the improper one."

"The bagel fell."

"You knocked it out of my hand," said Alvin.

"You shoved it in my face. You deserved what you got."

"That's exactly what I was thinking when I shoved it in your face."

The girl made a little *humpf*. "Then we're even."

"No, we're not. I'm hungry and you're the one with food. And, oh, I've got something to trade." Alvin took an Oreo out of his pack and gave it to her.

She looked at it, sitting there in her palm, as though it was a toad.

"Go on, eat it."

The girl turned her eyes away, but Alvin knew she wasn't looking at anything in particular. Something about the way she did it made her seem lonely.

"Go on," he said gently.

The girl took a bite. "It's mashed and crumbly."

"It still tastes good. Trade?"

The girl took the tin box out of her purse and gave Alvin a cinnamon bun. "Shouldn't you be in school today?"

"Shouldn't you?" He took a bite of bun, and the sweetness warmed him from head to toe. Everything suddenly seemed a whole lot better.

The girl closed the lid of the box carefully and put it away. "Are you traveling alone?"

Alvin grinned with his mouth full. "Not anymore."

CHAPTER TWELVE

The Border

Hardette pulled out a book. She gave Alvin an apologetic glance. "I'm in the middle of a really good part. I'll only read a chapter or two, okay?"

"Go ahead," said Alvin quickly. They'd been talking nonstop since they got on the train. He was glad to take a break.

Hardette was fourteen, which it turned out was old enough to ride the train alone, although she had to pay full fare. If she had been traveling with an adult, she would have had to pay only half—but alone, things were different.

She had bought him a ticket from New York to

Winnipeg—all eighty dollars coming out of his money—pretending he was her little brother. Because he was twelve, he could go half-fare with her.

At first he'd asked her to buy him a ticket all the way to Churchill. But she wasn't allowed to buy him a ticket for any farther than she was traveling; only an adult could buy him a ticket for the portion he'd have to travel alone.

The train companies had so many rules. And Hardette knew them all, because she'd been riding the train for years.

He glanced over at her book and read a few lines. He couldn't get any sense of what kind of book it was, but he was pretty sure it wouldn't interest him. He looked out the window at the world zipping by.

He was really here. A week ago he had no idea he'd ever be on a train to Canada. But now it seemed like everything he'd been reading and doing for a long time had prepared him for this. One thing had led to another, as though it was fated somehow. It was actually good that Mamma hadn't let him get the mountain bike, because if she had he wouldn't be here now.

And it was right for him to be here, watching the landscape as Hardette turned the pages of her novel. Everything he saw outside the window was new to him. It was unknown and scary and wonderful all at the same time. It was everything life should be.

He wrote on the postcard Hardette had given him. Then he leaned back and watched out the window.

When the train slowed for another station, Hardette pulled out the schedule and checked her watch. "Go on. According to the schedule, we stop in Buffalo for twelve minutes." She pointed under the printed line. Her finger bumped up and down with the motion of the train.

Alvin wanted to send the postcard to Mamma and Grandma. But if he got off the train, something might happen and he might not get back on in time.

Once they reached Canada, though, the American stamp Hardette had given him would be no good; he had to mail it now.

Mamma and Grandma were home, crying. As each mile had rolled by for the past eight hours, he had thought about them. "I'll jump off when the train stops." He stood in the aisle as the train gradually braked. "Should I bring my stuff? Just in case?"

"It'll slow you down." Hardette rubbed her hands together in worry. "Listen, take your money and your ticket. If you miss the train, I'll put your stuff in baggage check at the Toronto station under the name Alvin. I'll tell them you're coming to get it tomorrow. Okay?"

Alvin swallowed hard. "Good thinking." Hardette was smart; she always came up with an answer. And she was always calm.

He put the money sock in his jacket pocket with the ticket. The train's brakes squealed. He started down the aisle.

"Wait." Hardette ran after him and stuffed something into his hand. "Hurry up. Count in your head. If you reach three hundred and you haven't found a letter box, just run back."

Alvin almost smiled at how she said that about counting—as though he was a little kid—till he looked at the twenty dollars in his hand. "I can't take this. Anyway, I don't need it. You know I've got money."

"It's American money. I can't use it in Canada." Hardette looked out the window. "We're pulling in to track three. Remember that: three. Think of the people you've been telling me about: Grandma, Mamma, and you. Three. Track three. And count to three hundred." She pushed him. "Go on."

"That a memory exercise?" he asked. "Something you read about in your psychology books? Something for itty bitty kids?"

"Just don't forget. Go."

Alvin filed off the train with everyone else. A big olive green box shaped like a mailbox stood at the end of the track. But it turned out to be for something else. He spied a cafeteria inside the station and headed there, eyes scanning every direction. There was a gift shop across the central room, near the ticket windows. And a magazine and newspaper stand beside it. Then a doughnut shop. No mailbox.

And he realized he hadn't been counting. It might be a kid thing to do, but he had to admit it made sense—he should have done it. How long had he been gone? He ran across the huge room. No mailbox.

His teeth clenched. But, hey, all he really had to do was get someone to mail the card for him. That's all. He looked at the card. It read

> Dear Mamma and Grandma,
> How are you? I'm fine. Don't worry. Everything's going okay. I'm sorry I didn't call. But I'll write whenever I can. I'll be gone a while. Then I'll come home.
> Love, Alvin
>
> P.S. I love you.
> P.P.S. I took the Oreos. And the tuna fish.

There was nothing there that would make anyone suspicious. He could hand this postcard to any stranger and no one would give it a second thought.

A man walked by real close.

"Sir, please, sir." Alvin ran after him.

"What?" He was a short, skinny guy with a beard and glasses. He pulled out a dollar bill. "Here." He left.

Alvin stared at the money. It took a few seconds for it to make sense. His eyes stung. He thought of how his mother talked about the beggars on Mount Pleasant Street back home. He wanted to run after the man and give back the dollar. But his eyes passed the wall clock: 3:06. The train was scheduled to leave at 3:09.

Alvin ran back toward the tracks. He knocked into a little girl. He thrust the postcard at her with the dollar bill the man had given him. "Mail this for me."

"Mail the money?" said the little girl.

"Mail the postcard. The money's for you."

"What's going on?" A woman with a baby came toward them.

"Thanks, ma'am," he said as he ran past. "Pretty baby."

He was at the tracks now, running in the cold air.

Past track eight, seven, six, five. The train at track five started its engines. The sign said TORONTO: THE MAPLE LEAF. But that couldn't be right. The Maple Leaf should be on track three. He ran past track four. Track three was empty. Oh, no! No no no no no.

He ran back to track five, chanting no no no inside his head. This couldn't happen. Please no.

The doors were still open. A conductor stood outside the train. "All aboard!"

Alvin ran along the side of the train. Then he saw Hardette's head and arm sticking out a window way ahead. He jumped onto the nearest step and climbed into the train. The door closed automatically behind him, and the train left.

A woman leaned against the wall in the little entranceway of the car. "Close call." She laughed and took a drag on her cigarette.

Alvin stood splayed legged against the jerking movement of the train. He breathed deep and coughed on the cigarette smoke.

"Relax, kid. You made it. Where are you going anyway?"

"Toronto." That's where he had to change trains. He walked past the woman and made his way up aisle after aisle from car to car. Then he slid into the aisle seat beside Hardette. She took his hand and squeezed it. They leaned back.

"You told me track three," he said.

"It was track three, I swear. But after you got off, the train started moving and I ran to find a conductor. I thought we were leaving early. A passenger told me we were just changing tracks. I kept watch the rest of the time, so I could shout to you." She scratched her nose. "You sure took your time."

"I couldn't help it." The panic was only slowly letting go of Alvin's chest. After a long while, he took off his jacket and handed the twenty-dollar bill to Hardette.

She folded it tiny and stuck it back in her purse. "If we make it through customs, I'll buy you dinner in the dining car."

"If we make it through customs, we'll be in Canada," said Alvin. "You can't spend American money in Canada."

"You can spend American money anywhere."

"But you said . . . "

"I lied."

He laughed. The relief of having made the train had finally seeped in. He felt safe and happy and so grateful to be traveling with Hardette. "You bad, you know that?" Then he realized she was so strange, she might not understand. "Good bad, you know what I mean?"

A little kid across the aisle leaned toward them. "Hi." He had the bluest eyes Alvin had ever seen.

Alvin smiled. "Hi."

"Don't encourage him," whispered Hardette. "He got on while you were in the station and he blasted away on a metal fife until his mother stopped him. He's annoying."

As if to prove her point, the boy put the fife to his mouth and played one long loud note.

It was a pennywhistle. Wow.

That little boy would probably be really happy if he knew how to play the pennywhistle properly. Alvin smiled at him. "I can teach you a tune."

The boy clutched his pennywhistle to his chest and moved closer to his mother. The mother's eyes met Alvin's. She smiled and nudged the kid toward him. But the kid climbed past his mother and looked out the far window. The mother gave a little apologetic lift of the eyebrows.

Hardette's shoulder pushed against his. "Don't let him bother you," she said softly. "He's obviously a spoiled idiot." Then she giggled. "At least he's quiet now." She wiggled in her seat to get comfortable. "I don't really like my American cousins. They're spoiled too. And sloppy. I visit them every winter starting at the middle of Kwanzaa because my mother thinks that's the right thing to do. In Canada not too many people know about Kwanzaa yet. Anyway, my cousins always fix my hair like this." She ran her fingers through the beads at the tips of her cornrows. "They spend hours braiding one another's hair. All their friends do it too." She shook her head and the braids slapped on her cheeks. "I like it, don't you?"

"Yeah," Alvin said. "A lot."

Hardette smiled. "I thought all Americans were like them. But you're not." She took a candy stick out of her purse and broke it in half. The sweet smell of root beer filled the air. She handed Alvin half.

He sucked on the root-beer stick. It was exactly what he needed. It felt good to be sitting there on the train, lazy, with a mouth full of sugar. He enjoyed the gentle rocking. After a while he asked, "Want another Oreo?"

"Yech."

"I know what you mean." He put the Oreo bag under the seat. "I'll give them to the next homeless person I see."

"Hmmm," said Hardette, sucking away on the root-beer stick. She set her hand flat on the window and left a print.

"A man in the Buffalo station . . . " Alvin felt the blood rush into his cheeks again.

"What?" said Hardette. She looked at him.

"I stopped a man to ask him to mail the postcard. But he didn't give me a chance. He handed me a dollar."

Hardette shivered. "He probably thought he was being generous. He's an idiot, too."

Alvin bit a chunk off the candy and crushed it in his teeth.

"When I visit my aunt," said Hardette, "she treats me like . . . I don't know. My cousins are younger than me—six and nine. My aunt goes shopping, and she leaves me in charge of them. But not in a nice way. It's like I'm a nanny. And she acts like she's doing me a favor. She thinks of us as her poor relatives."

Alvin drew back in surprise. Everything about Hardette seemed refined. "Are you poor?"

Hardette moved her shoulders around, then

squared them. "My father works at the university."

"That doesn't sound poor to me."

"He's on the buildings and grounds crew." Hardette played with a braid. "We're not starving. Not like you. Is that why you're running away? Because you're hungry all the time?"

"I was only hungry because I ran away. Mamma makes enough money to feed us. She takes good care of us."

Hardette leaned closer. "So, why?"

"I told you before, it's necessary."

Hardette blinked. Then she sat back in her seat.

That was something really good about her: She accepted what he said. In fact, so far she'd been wonderful. He looked at her and realized how grown-up she seemed. Everyone always said Alvin was mature for his age, but Hardette beat him by far. "You go to high school, right?"

"I skipped a year, so I'm in grade ten." Hardette lifted her chin in that way that had made Alvin think she was prissy when he first met her this morning. But now it just seemed to be one of her habits. "My aunt says I'm old enough to do everything by myself. She sent me to the station alone on the suburban train because she had to go back to work this week. She didn't even say good-bye. She just left a ticket and the train schedule on the kitchen table."

"And the twenty dollars," said Alvin.

Hardette shrugged. "Yes."

"And the box of cinnamon buns and cheese sand-wiches." He thought fondly of the lunch they'd shared together on the train.

"No. My uncle bought the buns at the bakery for my cousins. I snuck a few without asking. And I made the sandwiches myself. I don't even like cheese, but that's all there was in the house."

"I love cheese," said Alvin.

The train slowed down as it neared another station.

"Niagara Falls. That's the last stop in the United States. Say good-bye to your homeland, Alvin."

He nodded. "Good-bye, homeland."

"And we better start Operation Border."

He glanced around. A few passengers stirred here and there, but no one was looking at him and Hardette. Okay, it was time. But just at that moment the woman with the boy stood up and fumbled around in the overhead rack for her luggage. She couldn't seem to get it down.

Alvin stood up. He was shorter than the woman. Still, he was strong and the woman's bag was small. "Can I help you?"

"Thank you. It's stuck."

He stood on the armrest and grabbed hold of the rack with his left hand. With his right he reached under her bag and found the problem—a hanging name tag had gotten twisted around the metal rail of the rack. He untwisted it, and the woman pulled the bag down just as the train came to a full stop.

The woman smiled hurriedly and turned to the boy. "Come on. Grab your pack."

The boy looked dazed; he'd clearly been asleep. He got on his knees and flailed around under the seat, coming up with a small, bright blue backpack. The woman took his hand.

"My flute," said the boy. "I lost my flute."

"We can't look for it now. We've got to hurry."

"I want my flute!" shouted the boy.

The woman pulled him down the aisle. "We'll buy another."

Alvin felt around the floor, then between the seat cushions. He was about to give up when he saw a flash of silver. The pennywhistle was jammed between the side of the seat and the window. He pulled it out.

But by then the woman and boy were gone. He ran to the window. The woman was rushing toward the stairs, holding the boy in her arms with his face buried in her neck. Within seconds she was lost from sight.

Alvin went back to his seat. He was glad to have the pennywhistle, but it felt odd, getting it that way. He hoped the mother would keep her promise and buy the little boy another.

Hardette tugged on his sleeve. "What's the matter? You don't really know how to play it, do you?"

"I learned in school."

"Your school must not be that bad, then. And your mom has a job." Hardette stared at him. "Alvin, you're going to have to tell me everything. You can't just keep saying this is necessary. I'm an accomplice. I have a right to know. I could get in a lot of trouble. I won't let you go on to Churchill alone unless I know what this is all about."

"If we make it over the border, I'll tell you. I promise."

"All right." Hardette stood up and moved past Alvin out into the aisle. "Be quick. We have to finish Operation Border before the new passengers get on."

Alvin dropped to the floor and wriggled around until he was stretched out with his head under Hardette's seat and his feet under the seat in front of that. The set of seats behind them was empty, so no one saw him do it. Hardette shoved his backpack under her seat from behind, to form a little wall that hid his head. Then she put her own suitcase on the floor, resting on its narrow end, between their seats, so that it made a barrier on Alvin's right side. His left side was against the train wall.

"Are you okay down there?" she whispered.

"Yeah."

Alvin felt something fall on his tummy. He knew it was his jacket. That's what they'd agreed on. Then he heard little squeaks above his face as Hardette climbed into her seat.

He felt a little more weight on his tummy. That had to be Hardette's feet. And now he felt her tucking thick cloth around his shins. She had opened his sleeping bag and spread it everywhere.

Suddenly most of the dim light under the seat was cut off. He knew that Hardette had draped her coat across her legs, so that it hung over her suitcase, too. Operation Border was complete. Alvin couldn't be seen from any direction. At least that's what they hoped, because that was important. While the regular train conductors simply looked at their tickets and moved on, the border control was unpredictable. Hardette said they always asked her questions. Just to be friendly. And they usually looked at passports. Alvin didn't have a passport. So they thought up Operation Border.

Hardette bounced around a little, then she stopped moving. She was pretending to be asleep, like they had agreed.

Alvin heard people getting on at both ends of the car. The smell of Oreos from the bag beside his head was strong.

By the time the train moved again, he was sweating. There were footsteps in the aisle, and voices. They stopped right beside Alvin and Hardette. Then they moved past.

Alvin's heartbeat returned to normal. But only for a little while; the train stopped a second time. They had passed into the Canadian side of Niagara Falls. This was the border check—and this was where he was most likely to get caught.

Footsteps in the aisle again. His left arm itched. And Hardette's feet had grown heavy on his stomach. Had she truly fallen asleep? If she had, what would happen when they woke her? What if she was startled? What if she sat up straight and let the coat fall and the sleeping bag slide away? Would they get arrested?

"Papers, please," said a loud voice from the aisle.

Hardette made a groggy noise. Alvin tightened his fingers around the pennywhistle. His breathing seemed loud, as though it echoed off the bottom of the seat.

"Toronto, is it?"

Hardette murmured assent.

"Are you ill?"

"What?" came Hardette's voice, slightly scared. "I'm fine."

"Why are you all wrapped up like that?"

Alvin almost choked. It was as though all the saliva in his mouth gathered at the back of his throat and threatened to suffocate him. He fought hard not to cough. Sweat rolled from the bridge of his nose down into his right eye. It stung.

"I—I'm chilly," said Hardette.

No one could be chilly on this train. Now the man would know Hardette was lying. He'd make her stand up. He'd catch Alvin.

But the footsteps and the loud voice moved on.

CHAPTER THIRTEEN

Psychology

At seven o'clock that night Alvin found himself in the dining car sitting across a linen tablecloth from Hardette, grinning till his cheeks hurt.

This was like traveling with a sister. Well, not that he knew what it would be like to have a real sister, but he bet that traveling with a real sister couldn't be any better than this.

Alvin's father and Uncle Pete used to travel together all the time. At least, whenever his father couldn't convince Mamma to go. Uncle Pete was Mamma's brother, not Alvin's father's brother. But they'd grown up neighbors—and best buddies, better than brothers.

They went on road trips to Atlanta and Nashville and New Orleans, because they both loved jazz, of course, and the blues, too.

Alvin never got enough of hearing Uncle Pete tell about the fun he and Alvin's father had had together. No one else ever talked about his father that way—freely and openly, as though memories couldn't hurt. Mamma still found ways to stop the conversation when it turned to Alvin's father.

Alvin knew more facts about Matthew Henson's life than he did about his own father's.

If his father hadn't died, Alvin would have traveled with him. They would have been best buddies. They would have seen the whole United States together.

But here he was traveling, all the same. And in Canada. Tonight was good. Tonight was very, very good. Tonight anything was possible.

They ordered roast chicken and peas and rice. Alvin was ravenous. "Food's okay," he said, about halfway through the meal.

"Swell," said Hardette.

No American kid would say "swell." But Hardette said it a lot, and by now he liked it.

She cut her chicken a little more forcefully. "So tell me. You promised."

"My mother . . . well, she's afraid of everything. Drugs and everything."

Hardette gave a little hiss. She stared at him. "Don't tell me you're into drugs. I never should have talked to you. I don't talk to strangers. But I made an exception. It's people like you who give bigots ammunition."

"I'm not into drugs. I swear," Alvin yelped. "Some dealer stopped me for a minute—and I walked away. But I made a mistake and told my mother about it. And that was all she needed. There was this big article in the newspaper right before Christmas about kids my age getting into drugs, so when my mother heard about this dealer she went nuts—because my mother always goes nuts—whatever bad thing can happen to a kid she always figures will happen to me—and she asked a neighbor to walk me to and from school so that no drug dealer could get me. To and from school, like a little kid."

Hardette looked incredulous. "You ran away because of that?"

"Come on, Hardette. I'm in sixth grade. Would you put up with that when you were my age?"

"Twelve's not that old."

"In my neighborhood it is."

"Yeah, I guess I know that. The kids in my cousins' neighborhood grow up pretty fast, too."

"And it was more complicated than that," said Alvin, "'cause a guy at school was ragging on me anyway. So it was going to get horrible fast."

"I know how that is." Hardette leaned forward over her plate. "Did you argue with your mother? Did you even try to change her mind?"

"Mamma doesn't change her mind. And besides, that's not the whole reason I left."

"Well?"

"Well, so many things. She won't let me have a mountain bike."

"A mountain bike?" Hardette's voice grew thin.

"Don't make it sound so dumb. I wanted it for Christmas. I was going to take a bike trip with my uncle this spring. We would have gone all over the countryside in Maryland. And I could have gone other places, too. Anywhere. All on my own. But my mother won't let me ride bikes. She won't let me spend the night at anyone's house. She wouldn't even let me go on the school trip to Williamsburg last year because the class stayed overnight." Alvin squashed a pea with his thumb. "And I had read more about Williamsburg than anyone else. I wanted to go more than anyone. I always want to go more than anyone. And she already said she won't let me go on the school trip this year, either. Matthew Henson was working on a ship by the time he was twelve. He went all over. But my mother won't even let me go on a class trip."

"Who's Matthew Henson?" said Hardette.

She'd never even heard of his hero. He put his hands on either side of his plate and looked her in the eye. "An explorer," he said. She didn't follow up. She didn't ask where Henson went exploring. She didn't care about exploring. If he talked about the North Pole, she'd think he was dumb. "Look, Hardette, I never get to go anywhere. You don't understand. Your parents send you to another country all by yourself. You can't understand." Alvin felt his face crumpling. He looked away.

Hardette reached across the table and touched his hand. "Maybe you could come home with me."

"That wouldn't solve anything. I want to go . . . " He couldn't finish. Hardette simply wouldn't get it. She didn't know what it was like not to be able to breathe because someone was always standing so close. She couldn't fathom the longing that was so palpable in his gut that he felt he'd die, just simply burst and die, if he couldn't get out and away fast. He turned his head. "Anyway, your parents might not want me."

"My father understands running away."

Alvin looked quick at Hardette. "Really?"

"He came to Canada to escape the draft. The Vietnam war and all. He was against it. But my mother . . . well, she does everything right. She might call your mother." Hardette shrugged. "So that won't work, after all. I'm sorry."

"Don't be. I want to go to Churchill."

"Why Churchill?"

"Why not Churchill?"

Hardette lifted her chin. "That's not an answer. Unless you're saying you could go anywhere else just as well. Could you? Why don't you turn around right now and go to Mexico instead? It's a lot nicer than Churchill in January."

"I don't want to go to Mexico. I'm going to Churchill."

Hardette's head gave a quick bob. "That's what I thought. Churchill is important. Then I can guess why you're going."

Alvin smiled in spite of himself. "Not in a zillion years."

"It's just a matter of using psychology." Hardette moved around in her seat, as though she was getting comfortable. That was another one of her habits that he knew by now. "Clue number one: You didn't get the mountain bike for Christmas."

"True." Alvin swallowed a forkful of peas. Hardette was a funny one.

"Clue number two: Your postcard said, 'Dear Mamma and Grandma.'"

"You weren't supposed to read my postcard." He ate the thin slice of orange that garnished the rice.

"I didn't. I just saw the beginning." Hardette drank her Coke. "Anyway, I don't have to use that clue. I could use the fact that all you've talked about was Grandma and Mamma, so that's who you live with." She took another sip. "Clue number three: You're only twelve, so you can't be following a lover."

Alvin wanted to laugh, but Hardette's face was serious. He gagged on the orange.

"Clue number four: You're a boy." She cut a chunk of chicken and chewed it thoughtfully. "There's only one answer."

"Only one answer?" Alvin was amazed.

"There are many logical answers. But there's only one answer that makes sense psychologically. And there's a second answer that doesn't really make sense, but it's consistent."

"Don't talk all that psychology junk. What's your answer?"

"Answer number one: You're going to find someone. Someone who will get you that bike."

Alvin started to shake his head.

"And I even know who." Hardette smiled. "Your father."

Alvin's mouth dropped open.

"Psychology books talk about how an adolescent boy needs his father. Your father's in Churchill, and you think you'll be better off with him." She stirred her peas around into her rice. "So, am I right?"

"My dad's dead."

"Oh." Hardette's eyes filled with tears. "I'm so sorry."

Alvin felt tears coming on just because of Hardette's. But that was silly. He never cried over his father. Sometimes he got sad at the idea of his father—at the idea of not having him—but that wasn't the same as crying about someone real to you, someone you actually missed. "You don't have to cry. I don't remember him. Not much, anyway. I was little. I was barely four." He cleared his throat. "There's no one waiting for me in Churchill."

Hardette nodded. She slowly ate a bite of the peas-and-rice mess. "Guess I blew that one. I want to go to university and study psychology. I've been reading books about it on my own for years, because my school doesn't teach it. But maybe I won't be so good at it."

"You'll be great at it."

She cut several small pieces of chicken and mixed them into the peas-and-rice mess.

"I thought you were fussy about eating," he teased, trying to make her feel better.

Hardette looked at him with surprise on her face.

"You know, how you didn't want me to eat my bagel because it fell on the floor. And now you made a big mess on your plate."

"It's a matter of nutrition," said Hardette. "The amino acids form better if you mix the food."

"It mixes inside you," said Alvin.

"It tastes good this way, too," said Hardette. "So your mom never got married again?"

"Nope."

"How old is she, anyway?"

"Twenty-seven."

"She had you when she was only one year older than me. Wow." Hardette took another bite. "My mom's old. And my dad's even older. So how old's your grandma?"

"She's not my grandma, really. My grandma ran off when my mother was little. My great-grandma raised my mother. But I call her Grandma, 'cause that's what Mamma calls her."

"Families," said Hardette. "They don't go in nice straight lines. I've got a pretty mixed-up family, too." She ran her finger along the edge of her plate. "How did your dad die?" she asked almost in a whisper.

"Mamma says he was in the wrong place at the wrong time."

"That's all you know?"

"Pretty much." Alvin expected Hardette to start quoting stupid stuff from her psychology books again. He expected her to say that his father's death was why his mother was so afraid all the time. It was obvious, even to him. He could feel himself getting worked up. There might be explanations for why Mamma acted like she did, but those explanations didn't make it any better. She had no right to wrap him up like some kind of doll, like a preserved mummy or something, and put him on a shelf forever. He got ready to fight Hardette.

But she didn't say anything.

They ate in silence.

Slowly Alvin calmed down. He was grateful that Hardette didn't press him now. He filled his mouth with rice and let the little grains soothe him.

"So why are you going to Churchill?" Hardette asked at last.

"I have to," Alvin said softly. "I just have to."

"That's what I thought," said Hardette. "That was my second guess. Psychologists talk about that, too. Sometimes it's just the beauty of the journey."

Alvin blinked in surprise; Hardette really was good. The fierce beauty.

CHAPTER FOURTEEN

The Last Train

Alvin couldn't have had better luck with the train schedules. It was Thursday evening when he said good-bye to Hardette, and one of the only three trains a week that went from Winnipeg to Churchill was leaving at ten.

Hardette cried when they parted. Alvin cried too. They had spent most of the day with him teaching her to play the pennywhistle. He wanted to give it to her when they parted—but that made her cry more. She promised to buy herself one soon.

In their time together, it had felt more and more like they were brother and sister. Or what Alvin imagined brothers and sisters felt like. They'd even had a brief argument over which was a better game, soccer or ice hockey. It was a stupid argument, because he had never even seen a live ice hockey game, much less played it. But brothers and sisters had stupid arguments all the time, didn't they? He loved it. Hardette gave him her address and made him promise to write and let her know how everything turned out.

Alvin had a stomach full of meatballs from lunch, which Hardette had insisted on paying for. She had shared her breakfast with him, too. And she'd given him her toothpaste.

In his backpack, besides the can of tuna, were two sandwiches, a pack of pretzels, and two cans of apple juice that he'd bought on the train.

His teeth were clean, he was well fed and well slept, he had food in his pack and money in his pocket. There were only two things he needed now: someone to help him buy a ticket to Churchill and a safe place to pass the time till ten o'clock.

The most promising place was the waiting room. He settled himself at the end of a row of seats and rested his head against the wall. From here he could see everyone who entered.

The room was reasonably full. Still, there was no one he felt safe approaching about a ticket. No one old enough to do it but not so old that he'd ask a lot of questions and maybe call the police.

A young man leaned on a trash can. He fiddled with keys. He had a stubble of red-brown beard, and his jacket hung lopsided and tattered. Everything about him seemed shabby and lost.

Did Alvin look shabby and lost? Only a moment ago he had felt pretty good, but now doubt overtook him. This was so hard—this business of traveling. He missed Hardette. At least together they could laugh and nothing seemed really that bad. Traveling with her took the edge off. But now he was alone again. Really alone.

In a foreign country.

Sadness made his shoulders slump. He was tired. He wanted to relax totally. To sleep for a long time in his own bed.

How were Mamma and Grandma? Had they got-ten his postcard?

At least he had written them a real letter now. He told them about the countryside outside the window of the train. And about Hardette. No details—he couldn't let them figure out where he was—but enough so that they'd know he was safe. Hardette had taken the letter and promised to find someone headed for America and ask them to drop it in the mail once they crossed the border. That way no one would trace the letter and find out he was way up in Canada. He would write them again from Churchill and get someone who was going back on the train to mail it for him from wherever they got off. And he'd write to Hardette, too. He patted the pocket that had the napkin with her address on it.

He closed his eyes.

Grrrr.

Alvin jumped to his feet.

A man in the next row of seats, halfway down, snored loudly.

Alvin was used to snoring because of Grandma. He missed her now. He missed how she could laugh at Mamma's rules, getting around them in a way he'd never quite learned.

He opened his jacket and stood to try to cool off a bit. He picked up his backpack and sleeping bag and walked around the waiting room. Voices came from somewhere in the station. Alvin crossed the main hall toward the noise. He entered a food court and sat down at one of the tables in the center of the room. He wasn't sleepy anymore. He had the jitters.

And he needed to cool down. This station had the heat up too high. He opened his backpack in preparation for taking off a sweatshirt, but the sight of the pennywhistle stopped him. He rubbed it with his bare hands.

"Not on your life."

Alvin looked around quickly.

A middle-aged woman with a black-and-white checked scarf tied under her chin sat down at the table behind him. "You play that pipe, kid, and I'll break it." The woman put her paper plate on the table and stuffed the last of a doughnut into her mouth. Her olive skin seemed sallow, as though she was sick. She looked familiar. "Here." She held out two paper bills. "I've got to get through the night in this bleak country with some semblance of peace. Take the money and keep quiet."

Alvin looked at the two Canadian dollars.

The woman leaned toward him. "Are you telling me a little urchin like you doesn't know how to grab money?"

Alvin looked at her yellow-and-brown teeth.

The woman put the money on Alvin's table. She loosened her kerchief. Then she took a cigarette out of her purse and lit up. Alvin suddenly knew where he'd seen her before. And at the same moment, she recognized him. "You're the kid who almost missed the train back in—where was it?—way back in Buffalo, right?" The woman looked at Alvin slyly. "You said you were going to Toronto. Now here you are in Winnipeg. Something's going on with you. I knew it the first minute I laid eyes on you." Her tone was malevolent.

Alvin stood up and pointed the pennywhistle at her. "If you bother me, I'll blow this in your ear the second you fall asleep."

The woman did a mock shiver. "Ooo, you scare me, shorty." She put out her cigarette. "I've got a mind to turn your sorry ass over to the cops. Who knows what kind of trouble you're in. And dressed like you are, I'd probably be doing you a favor."

Alvin spun on his heel and ran, back into the main station hall and straight to the men's room. He washed his face in the sink. It wasn't that dirty and he wasn't dressed that poor; the woman was wrong: He didn't look like an urchin. He dried himself with paper towels. Then he collapsed in a corner.

• • •

An argument close by woke him. He stepped into a stall and took care of business. What was the matter with him? He kept falling asleep—as though he was sick or something. He walked past the three arguing men and looked out into the station hall. The wall clock read 21:52. What? Then he remembered that the train schedule on the website had been on the twenty-four–hour system. So the clock was too. Okay, that meant it was 9:52 p.m.

His train left in only eight minutes.

He scanned the signs. The train for Churchill was at track two. There was no time to find someone to help him buy a ticket. Somehow he'd have to buy one on board.

He ran outside to the platforms. The blast of cold air hit him full body. His fingers scrambled to zip up his jacket. He'd never felt cold like this before. And the air was different—thin and empty and wild. The electric lights on the train platforms made everything under them bright, while the world outside their sphere was pitch black. The track in front of him was number five, but he could see his train at track number two. It was short: only two passenger cars and three freight cars.

"Hey." The kerchief woman pointed at Alvin and

shouted, "Stop!" She waved her arms toward a man with a red hat. "Stop that boy."

Alvin jumped onto the train at track five. He looked out a window. The man in the red hat huddled with the woman in the kerchief. She pointed to the train Alvin was on.

Alvin ran the length of the car. He had to get out before the Churchill train left without him. But if he got off this train on the same side, the man in the red hat would see. He tried to open a window on the side of the train away from the loading platform. It didn't move. He tried the window on the door in the little corridor between train cars. It slid up easily. He looked down. It was a long drop to the ground, and then he'd have to be careful not to land on the rails. A skull and crossbones was painted on the inside of the platform right above the rails.

"What's he doing?" A woman spoke loudly to the man beside her. "What's that boy doing?" The man was busy pulling a wrapper off a plate of food. He didn't lift his eyes.

Alvin looked at the woman and put his finger to his lips to signal hush. He ran back to the loading side and looked out the window again. The man in the red hat was talking to another man in a red hat.

A third man in a red hat rushed toward them.

Alvin ran back to the window over the track on the other side. What if another train pulled in right as he was jumping out? He leaned out the window and looked as far as he could see. No train in sight. He threw his sleeping bag out.

The woman pointed at him now with a shaking finger. "Look, Roger. Look what he's doing."

Alvin waved good-bye. Then, with a sudden surge of feeling, he blew a kiss, climbed out, and hung from the window top. He dropped close to the train, as far from the next set of rails as he could.

Pain shot through his right ankle. He fell backward onto his bottom. The heels of both hands hit the ground. They stung. But he got up quick. The noise of an engine came from beyond the train he'd just jumped out of; the Churchill train was revving up. He limped around the end of the train and hoisted himself up onto the loading platform. He hurried like a madman to track two and jumped onto a passenger car.

A man in a red hat came down the aisle. Alvin jumped off the train, ignoring the throb in his ankle, and ran past the second passenger car to the first freight car. The door was open. He looked around. Two men in red hats were hurrying to the other train. If he didn't act fast, they'd see him. He slipped off his backpack and threw it into the car. That's when he realized his sleeping bag was still on the rails over at track five. But there was no time now. He got into the freight car, grabbed his pack, and climbed over wooden crates. Someone pulled the sliding door of the freight car shut—*bang*—from the outside. Within seconds, the train was in motion.

It was totally dark inside. The crate under Alvin wobbled. He felt his way back to the small open area in front of the door and sat on the metal floor. It was ice cold, but at least it was stable. The roar of the wheels deafened him.

He was all alone in the dark. He clutched his backpack as tight as he could. The train jerked and a crate toppled onto his right leg, the one with the hurt ankle. He tried to push it off, but it was too heavy. He managed to pull his leg out and edge closer to the door.

His stomach tightened in hunger. He ate the ham sandwich he'd bought on the last train and drank one of the cans of apple juice. He felt better. Just cold.

Thin lines of tightness pulled on his cheeks. He realized he was crying. He shouldn't be crying. Everything was okay. He was on his way to Churchill.

Plus it was better that he was in a freight car. Now he wouldn't have to hassle over buying a ticket.

And even though he hadn't paid for this trip, it wasn't really like stealing, because he'd try to find a way to buy a ticket when he got off and then he'd give it to someone who really needed it. Maybe someone like that shabby guy in the Winnipeg waiting room. Wouldn't the person be surprised? The idea made him smile. But smiling hurt his lips.

There was no heat in the freight car.

Alvin knew freight cars didn't have heat, but he hadn't thought about that when he jumped in. The reality of that fact, the implications of it for the trip ahead, shocked him. His fingers stiffened and his ears ached. He felt inside his backpack for gloves. He found one and put it on, but he couldn't find the other in the dark. He put two socks on the other hand and pulled on his new wool hat, rolling it down over his ears. He'd been annoyed that Mamma had bought it so big it didn't fit right—but now he was glad. It came down the sides of his head, all the way to his neck.

The metal floor hurt his butt, it was so cold. He sat on his backpack and buried his hands in his armpits. He needed to go to the bathroom, but the thought of unzipping his pants in this frigid air unnerved him.

He remembered the train schedule precisely: This train would pull into Churchill on Saturday morning at seven thirty.

The ride was thirty-three and a half hours.

That's what the woman in the kerchief meant when she said "dressed like that." She wasn't saying he was dressed poor, she was saying he wasn't dressed for this kind of cold. She was saying he'd be better off in a jail.

After at least an hour, the train stopped. Alvin heard voices. He got up as fast as his cramped legs could make it and walked to the door. He would switch to a heated passenger car now.

He tugged at the inside handle on the door. It didn't move. He threw all his weight against it, over and over. But the door didn't open. The train started up again.

He gasped.

Well, how long could it be till the next town? Not so long. No. Passengers would be getting off and they'd need their stuff, right? The door would open from the outside. It had to.

He climbed onto a crate and perched there, as far from the cold floor as he could get. He stayed there through the next stop, and the one after that. And another. And another. He lost count, there were so many, so close together.

The door never opened.

Passengers had their luggage with them in the passenger cars. These crates were something else. How far were they going? Maybe the end of the line.

He couldn't think that way. He'd lose his mind if he did.

He got colder and colder. He opened his pack and put his sweatpants over his jeans. Then he took off his jacket and put on his extra sweatshirt and put his jacket back on. All the clothing left in the pack now was socks, underwear, and the glove he couldn't find before. He took the two socks off his hand and put on the glove.

The pain in his feet made him clench his teeth. He had to get them warmer, but he knew he wouldn't be able to fit them back in his sneakers if he put more socks on. He tried to pull a sock over his shoe—it didn't work. So he tied two socks around the outside of each sneaker. Every layer counted. That left one pair of socks and three pairs of underwear.

Alvin was out of breath simply from dressing himself. He didn't know how long he'd been in the train car, but he realized there hadn't been any stops for a long time. What if there were no more stops till the end?

He had never been this cold in his life. He could barely think—it was as though his brain was freezing. Whenever the train stopped again, he would bang on the doors and shout. Even if they arrested him for being a stowaway, that would be okay. Jails had heat. The woman in the kerchief was right.

The train rolled on.

He opened the second can of apple juice. Nothing came out. It was frozen solid. He gnawed at his second sandwich; it was hard as a dog biscuit. The pain in his hands was excruciating. He put his hands in front of his mouth and exhaled on them, so his internal heat would warm whatever skin on his face was still exposed.

Terror seized him. He screamed.

When he stopped, he tasted blood. His mouth

was so cold that the corners had ripped when he opened it wide to scream.

He had to think about something—something that would heat his blood. He remembered the dog back home—the one behind the wood fence on Park Road that always barked and scared him into running till he panted. Then he thought of Matthew Henson driving a dog team—one that pulled a big sled with long wooden runners, called a sledge. The word stuck in Alvin's head because it seemed wrong, as though it was a mistaken way of saying "sled." He thought of how the Eskimos loved Henson for that— Ootah, Egingwah, Seegloo, and Ooqueah. And how Henson loved them back. That was probably why both the Eskimos and the dogs were on the bronze insets in Henson's memorial—he must have loved them.

Alvin thought about the words on Henson's memorial. The sheet of paper with those words was folded into his notebook inside his backpack. He'd made sure it was there before he left home.

He couldn't remember the words now. He knew them, he did—but they were gone. In fact, he couldn't remember the names of the four Eskimos. They were in his head a moment ago, one second ago, but they were gone now, too. Everything about Henson was gone.

His brain was too cold to think.

His nose felt like a knife, jabbing deep into his skull. He tied his scarf higher around his face. The pain in his feet was unrelenting, even with the socks tied around the shoes. He tucked them under him and sat that way for a while, but it was too hard to keep his balance with the jerking motion of the train. So he straightened his legs out in front of him again. His hands ached something horrible, even tucked under his armpits. He opened the pack, took off his hat, put the three pairs of underwear on his head, then forced the hat over them all. He dumped his money out of one of the remaining socks into the bottom of his pack. He pulled those socks onto his hands, over his gloves. He didn't feel any warmer. Slowly, though, everything stopped hurting.

Alvin was quietly going numb.

And he didn't have to go to the bathroom anymore. That was one good thing.

Only something nagged at the back of his mind—not terror anymore—just a vague worry—something about the numbness you feel before you freeze to death. He couldn't stay here like this. He had to do something.

He half crawled, half rolled off the crate. He couldn't straighten up, and he walked all stumbly with those socks around his shoes. He jiggled at the locks on two trunks, pulled at the ropes on so many crates.

Then he remembered the knife in his pack. The best pocketknife in the world. His father's knife. He got it now and cut through the ropes on a crate. But the crate was stuck shut.

He felt his way around the car again. A long cardboard box about three feet high sat under some crates. He jammed the knife into the center of the side of it. It went in. He must have hit a hollow spot inside. He cut a hole large enough to reach in. He took the sock and glove off one hand and felt. His hand was so cold and the stuff inside the box was so cold that he couldn't be sure—but maybe it was plastic wrapping. He put the glove and sock back on and slowly sawed away at the cardboard with his knife. He knew he should be doing it fast, but he couldn't do anything fast. Finally the hole was big enough for him to crawl into. He wedged himself in so that he was lying between the cardboard and the plastic wrapping.

Plastic wrapping was good insulation against the cold. His mother tacked up plastic over the windows on the back porch at home to keep out the winter winds. He'd be okay if he could just get inside that plastic wrapping.

He jabbed it with the knife. He took off his glove and felt under the wrapping. Cloth. He pushed hard. It seemed to give way a little. If only he could fit himself between the cloth and the plastic. He cut a long slit in the plastic. Then he poked in his legs and wriggled and wriggled and wriggled. Everything took so long. Everything took all his energy.

He was in up to his chest now, lying on his back on the cloth thing with the plastic tight around both of them. He turned his head away from the hole in the cardboard box. He could hear Mamma inside his head, worrying he'd suffocate. He turned his face back toward the hole.

He realized that he'd left his pack on top of the crate. That's where his only remaining food was. But it didn't matter because he couldn't imagine ever being hungry again. All he wanted was to be warm. It was so cold.

The sound of the door opening woke him. Light invaded—a large circle of light. Alvin worked to move his arm. He wanted to stick his hand out and hail whoever was there. But he was so stiff and he was jammed in so tight, he couldn't move.

A man stood in the open area by the door. He had his back to Alvin. The man's breath formed a cloud in the frigid air.

Alvin tried to call to him, but his voice wouldn't come.

The man pulled at a crate and shoved it toward the door. A man on the loading platform took it from him.

Alvin managed to get out a croaking noise. But the scrape of the crate across the floor of the car drowned it out.

Still, the man turned around. He squinted into the dark. "I heard something," he said to the man outside.

"We've got three more crates to unload. Hurry up."

The man turned his back on Alvin and read the label on a crate. He pushed it toward the door. Then he found another crate, and another. The man jumped out. The door slid shut.

Alvin closed his eyes. He wasn't even sad. He didn't care.

The train rolled on.

CHAPTER FIFTEEN

Churchill

Alvin could hear people. They sounded far away and he didn't catch what they were saying, but they were people, for sure. And suddenly he cared again. His heart beat so hard it hurt his ribs. He cried out. His voice came this time. Still, it took all his energy to make that one cry for help.

The voices got closer. Someone kept saying he heard something. If only Alvin could cry out again.

Then he was tilted sharply. They were lifting the box he was in, that had to be it. And someone had gone around past the box and was calling out into the back part of the train car, asking who was there.

Alvin realized his chest and back were wet. His body heat had caused condensation inside the plastic cocoon. He was chilled to the bone, but he wasn't frozen. He took the deepest breath he could manage and shouted.

Slam!

Alvin fell with a jolt. They must have dropped the box.

And now he could hear ripping and shouts.

Eyes looked right at his.

He shut his own in gratitude.

His feet woke him. They stabbed, like pins and needles, only worse. Alvin opened his eyes and looked around. He was in a small room, lying on a sofa, with a wool blanket pulled up to his chin. No light came through the one high window. But a desk lamp gave off a dim glow. The desk had a phone and stacks of papers on it and a computer. Against the wall were filing cabinets. On the floor by the sofa was his backpack, with the flap hanging open.

Alvin pushed himself up on his elbows. Weakness overcame him. He shut his eyes again.

• • •

The next time he woke, a man was sitting at the desk with his back toward him. Pale light filtered through the window and across the man's hand as he stirred something in a cup. Steam spiraled up from it. Near the door, on a large hook, hung an animal-hide parka and thick breeches. Fur-covered boots sat on the floor with hide mittens on top of them.

The smell from the cup overpowered Alvin. He tried to sit up. His stomach rebelled, and he retched. "Excuse me," he said, letting himself lie flat. His voice came out raspy. His lips felt funny. He touched them. They were greasy. He could smell it: Vaseline. Someone had Vaselined his lips, all the way around, even in the corners, over the bumpy scabs that had formed from his screaming before. "Excuse me," he said again.

"So you're finally awake." The man pushed back his chair and turned to face Alvin. He had black hair, black eyes, and a flat, round face. He got up. He must have been no more than five feet tall. Alvin remembered reading that nothing in the Arctic grew taller than five feet. He thought they were talking about the plants. After all, the dwarf willows were only a foot high. He hadn't realized they meant people too. And he wasn't even as far north as the Arctic yet. He couldn't be any farther north than Churchill, because that was the end of the train line.

The man left the room and came back a moment later with another cup. He sat on the sofa beside Alvin and put a spoon to Alvin's lips. Chicken broth. It was delicious. The man fed him slowly, saying nothing.

When the broth was gone, the man put the empty cup on the desk and sat in the chair. "What's your name?"

The hot broth in Alvin's stomach seemed to thaw every part of him. He looked into the patient eyes of this man.

"Come on," the man said quietly. "I have to call you something."

"Call me Pete." Uncle Pete wouldn't mind Alvin borrowing his name for a while.

"Pete what?"

Alvin shrugged.

"Is that your real name?"

Alvin looked away.

"What's your real name?" asked the man.

"What's your real name?" asked Alvin.

The man seemed to think about that. "When a stranger comes to town, I introduce myself as

Martin. But just like you, I've got two names. The church named me Martin. But my Inuk *Hanayuq* came first. I looked into his eyes and smelled his strong breath and I was so happy when he called me Manitok."

"Who's your Inuk *Hanayuq*?"

"The person who named me. I was born in Baker Lake. Everyone in my town has someone who names him. He takes the newborn in his hands and holds him up to his face and gives a name that suits his character."

Alvin gave a little laugh. "If you were a newborn, you can't say what you smelled and how you felt. You can't remember."

"I remember being born."

Alvin would have objected, but what was the point? This man was crazy if he thought he could remember being born. Still, Alvin felt a pinch of envy. He couldn't even remember his father, and people always say it's easy to remember when you were four. But he didn't, no matter how hard he tried. Sometimes, though, he felt like he missed him, a thick feeling in his chest, almost as if he remembered.

"So," said Manitok, "that's my real name, the one

my mother calls me by." He wrote on a yellow pad. "We found no papers on you. Just a mostly empty notebook. Where do you come from, Pete?"

"Far away." Alvin touched the corners of his mouth gingerly. They were starting to hurt. "Does 'Manitok' have a meaning, then, if your name is supposed to suit your character?"

"I was named after my uncle, who was sensible. I don't know how he was named." Manitok put down his pencil. "Looks like we better talk later. Tell me how you feel."

"Fine."

Manitok regarded him a moment. "Pete came to Churchill and pretty near froze to death, but he feels fine." He shook his head. "Who told you that outfit would get you through a Churchill day? It's January. You'd freeze to death in May in that."

Alvin swallowed. So it was true. It wasn't just him panicking—he had almost frozen on that train. He thought of defending himself, of saying that he'd planned on getting better clothes once he got far enough north, that the freight car had taken him by surprise. But what was the point? It didn't really matter what Manitok thought of him.

Manitok slapped his fingers on the yellow pad. "If

you hadn't managed to crawl under the plastic wrapping on Tracie's new couch, you'd be history by now. That's what Olayuk said, the doctor. Instead you're whole and healthy. You're lucky. Lots of people came in to see you when you were sleeping—everyone's curious—and they all agree: Someone somewhere must be on your side."

That sounded like something Grandma would have said. She would have put her arms around Alvin and squeezed him tight and said something just like that. He stretched. "I have to go to the bathroom."

Manitok helped Alvin get up. Then he wrapped the blanket around Alvin's shoulders and walked beside him into a medium-sized room and across to the door marked WASHROOM. Alvin limped a little. His ankle still hurt.

Once inside, Alvin looked out the window on white everywhere. The snowdrifts reached clear to the sill. The cold outside horrified him. But it was warm inside. It was warm.

He was alive.

All he had to do to stay alive was tell Manitok who he was. Then he could go home, where the coldest day of winter would never bother him again. He could stay safe forever. Safe and small, in a small, small world.

Better safe than sorry.

That's something Mamma would have said. She would have told him to be grateful he hadn't died for his foolishness. What was the point of spending his money on a long trip to nowhere, for no reason? He could hear her logical voice. She would hold it steady. She would make a list of rules for him to follow so that he'd never run a risk like this again.

And maybe she'd be right. Maybe he had gone overboard. Maybe all he really wanted was to get some rights for himself. Maybe exploring was a dream. A dumb dream.

Exploring.

There used to be so many explorers. Were they all dumb?

He stared at the snow. It looked deceptively soothing, as though it could cradle you.

"Come home, Alvin," whispered Mamma in his ear. "Come get warm. And safe."

If Matthew Henson had listened to advice like the kind Mamma always gave, he'd have quit after the first failed expedition.

Someone somewhere was on Matthew Henson's side, too.

Alvin cupped his hands and drank hot water from

the faucet. The ferocity of his thirst surprised him. He drank and drank. The more he drank, the stronger he felt.

He came back out into the medium-sized room. The cold of the floor penetrated through his socks. This was apparently the main room of the train station. A machine that sold hot drinks stood against one wall. That's where his chicken broth must have come from. There were crates stacked up in a corner. Probably the couch that had saved him was now in Tracie's house, whoever Tracie was.

A young man in cowboy boots and a broad-brimmed hat sat on a bench, smoking. Alvin wondered if his feet would freeze outside in those boots. Manitok was speaking to the man. When he saw Alvin, he took him by the elbow and led him back into the little room.

"You're American, right?" asked Manitok.

Alvin sat on the sofa and wrapped himself in the blanket.

Manitok sat facing Alvin in the desk chair without moving at all. He seemed almost like a statue. "How old are you, Pete?"

Alvin pulled his feet up so he was sitting campfire style. He remembered how Robert Peary had frostbite.

He rubbed his toes through his socks. They were all there.

"Are you running away?"

Alvin kept rubbing his toes.

"This is serious, you know, Pete. We're going to have to get you back home."

He wouldn't go back home. Or, at least, not without a struggle. He could get farther north than this, he knew he could. He still had plenty of money.

"You're in trouble," Manitok said. "If you cooperate, if you talk, it might not be as bad."

Alvin looked at the sincere face of Manitok. It was a very different face from his own. He thought of how the Eskimos accepted Matthew Henson. "Do I look like an Eskimo to you?"

"Watch your language. Saying 'Eskimo' is taken as a racial slur around here. I'm an Inuk."

"Oh." Alvin flushed. "Sorry, I didn't know."

"Now you do."

"Are all Inuks your color?" said Alvin.

"We vary. There's been a lot of intermarriage. And we say one person is an Inuk, but more than one are the Inuit. There's no *s* on the end—just the Inuit."

"The Inuit thought Matthew Henson looked just like them."

"Inside your notebook there's a computer-page printout of this Matthew Henson's grave," said Manitok. "Who was he?"

"A man," said Alvin.

"Someone you knew?"

"Sort of," said Alvin. "Is that man out there American?"

Manitok blinked. "You mean the cowboy?"

"Yeah." Alvin smiled. "The cowboy."

Manitok finally broke a smile in return. He seemed almost friendly. "He's from Chicago. He came to buy furs."

"From you?"

Manitok laughed. He had white, white teeth, and Alvin liked his laugh. "He's come to meet a trapper from the north. Trappers around Churchill get ordinary pelts, but this trapper goes up past the Arctic Circle, where the white Arctic foxes and hares are abundant and unafraid of people."

"Does he go by dog sledge?"

"Dog sledge?" Manitok really laughed now. "Almost no one in Canada uses sledges anymore. People use Ski-doos."

"Ski-doos?"

"Snowmobiles," said Manitok.

"So the cowboy is waiting for a Ski-doo?"

"No." Manitok looked at Alvin curiously. "He's waiting for the plane from Pangnirtung."

"Where's that?"

"Baffin Island."

The skin on the back of Alvin's neck tingled. Baffin Bay was where that man and his wife drowned in a kayak. But it was also the bay Matthew Henson went up to get to Ellesmere Island. It was a step along the way—one important step. "Is that far?"

Manitok stood up and furrowed his brow. "I'm the one who's supposed to be asking questions." He held his arms by his sides. They were short arms. His legs were short too. But the trunk of his body was like a barrel. "Don't go getting ideas about Pangnirtung. You wouldn't last half a day there."

The phone rang. Manitok picked it up. He spoke in a language Alvin couldn't understand. He said repeatedly, *"Nalujara."* At one point he said, "Matthew Henson." Manitok got off the phone and sank into the desk chair with a sigh.

"What's *nalujara* mean?"

Manitok looked surprised. "You're smart."

"What's it mean?"

"I don't know."

"You said it. You have to know."

"It means 'I don't know.' Navja asked questions about you. All I could say was *nalujara*. She isn't happy about that." Manitok picked his teeth with his fingernail. "Everyone wants to know more about you."

Navja was probably a cop. Alvin put his feet on the floor and pulled his backpack toward him. "Where's my sneakers?"

Manitok leaned down and pulled them out from under the sofa. "You can't go far in these."

"I only want to walk around the station. I'll stay inside."

"Leave your jacket here."

Alvin tied his laces and walked out into the main room. He went right to the cowboy. "Can you tell me when the trapper's coming, sir?"

The cowboy looked down his nose at Alvin. "Why?" He threw his cigarette butt on the floor and let it burn.

"I want to talk to him."

The cowboy scratched his chin. "He's not due in till one."

Alvin looked at the wall clock. It must be law that every train station have a wall clock. It was eleven twenty. Underneath it was a sign that read SATURDAY.

Alvin had been sleeping pretty much constantly since getting on the train Thursday night. Amazing.

He looked back at the cowboy. "You just going to waste time till he gets here?"

"This is my second trip to Churchill, and from what I can tell, anybody who comes here wastes time." The cowboy made a grimace. "Two thousand people live here and in the winter you'd think there was no one, the way they hole up."

"It's cold out."

The cowboy laughed. "Now aren't you the genius? Anyway, I'm going on a sightseeing trip at eleven thirty."

What could a sightseeing trip mean? All Alvin had seen out the window was snowdrifts. "A man can freeze dressed like you."

"Now what'd I say? A real genius. It's a heated bus." The cowboy pushed out his cheek with his tongue and looked sideways at Alvin. "You didn't know that, now did you, big guy?"

Alvin stood tall. It was okay when his friends called him Dwarf, but he didn't like this cowboy calling him big guy. "I never took a bus. I like to do my sightseeing walking."

"You're fun, big guy." The man laughed and

shook his head. "Go see polar bears walking—now that's an idea."

Hardette had said Churchill was polar bear country. But she couldn't have meant in winter. "Bears hibernate."

"They better not. I already paid." The cowboy stamped his boot and cursed. "That bus tour promised polar bears."

Now that Alvin thought about it, none of this made sense. "You can't go far. There are no roads out of Churchill."

The cowboy cursed again. He took a pack of Marlboros out of the inside pocket of his jacket. He lit a cigarette. Then he looked at Alvin steadily. He held out the pack, offering.

Alvin stared at it.

The cowboy grinned. "See, you ain't such a big guy." He put the pack in his pocket. "You're just playing games. If I wasn't so bored, I'd tell you to shut up."

Alvin opened his mouth to protest. Then he smiled back. This cowboy didn't treat him like he was a little kid. He might be okay, after all.

The cowboy settled back on the bench and looked comfortable. "So, buddy, why're you waiting for Steve?"

"Steve?"

"I thought you said you were waiting for the trapper."

Alvin flexed his fingers. All the feeling had come back finally. "I didn't know his name."

"You're looking to make money with him, huh?"

Alvin nodded noncommitally.

"You should be in school."

Alvin didn't nod.

The cowboy laughed. "At your age I wasn't such a scholar myself."

Manitok came in and walked over to Alvin. "I have to go home. I'll bring you back a sandwich. Don't disappear on me."

A sandwich. Hunger clenched Alvin's stomach. "I won't, sir. Thank you, sir."

"Good."

"He's coming to see polar bears with me," said the cowboy.

Alvin tensed up. "I didn't say that."

"Are you afraid?" The cowboy smirked.

Of course he was. "I got no money for a sight-seeing bus." It was true: The rest of his money had to go for a plane ride with the trapper.

"I figured as much," said the cowboy. "Don't worry about it. I could use the company."

Manitok looked placidly at the cowboy. "Polar bear tours are in October and November."

"Why? Do they hibernate?" asked the cowboy belligerently.

"Not most of them. In the coldest part of winter some of them stay in snow caves. But generally they hunt all the time. That's all they do: hunt." Manitok kept looking at the cowboy.

"So why are the tours in the fall?" asked the cowboy.

"Most people don't like to visit when it's this cold."

The cowboy nodded. "I have to come whenever the coat factory sends me. So I might as well see some bears."

Manitok shrugged. "I haven't seen a polar bear for weeks. Seem scarce these days."

"What?" The cowboy stood up. "I paid a guy twenty bucks to see polar bears. He didn't say nothing about them being scarce."

"Who did you pay?"

"Some jerk Eskimo."

Alvin looked quickly at Manitok. But Manitok's eyes remained placid.

The cowboy shuffled his feet and sat down. "The guy had some crazy long name."

"Taitsianguaraitsiak?" said Manitok.

"Yeah. That's it."

"He knows polar bears. If he said you'll see one, then he knows where one is."

The cowboy scratched his chin. "He better." His voice rose a little as he warmed to his subject. "This better be a good tour. And I better not get cold."

"If you stay inside the bus," said Manitok in a soft, even voice, "you'll be okay in your jacket." He looked at Alvin now. "Go on. Get it. And your hat and gloves."

Alvin hesitated. But he'd be in a bus. And Manitok had a sensible character. And the whole point of this trip was to see things—whatever there was to see wherever he went. Mamma wasn't here—and polar bears were.

He ran into the office and put on his jacket. He stuck his hands in the pockets almost instinctively. They were empty. He searched through his pack. He found his gloves, hat, and scarf, along with the extra clothes he had pulled on in the freight car. They were folded neatly. His money was at the bottom of the pack. But nowhere did he find what he was looking for: the napkin with Hardette's address. She'd written it down in the dining car. It must have fallen out somewhere along the way.

The pang of loss made Alvin press his hands to his head. Having her address mattered; he felt more alone without it. He should have copied it into his notebook, like he'd planned to.

But actually, it was good that her address wasn't on him when Manitok found him. Otherwise they would have contacted her, and then they'd have found out where he was from and that would have been the end of everything.

So it was okay. Everything was okay.

Just like it was okay that Mamma hadn't gotten him the bike. Everything was turning out as it should. All Alvin had to do was let it happen.

When he came out of the room, the cowboy was gone. He ran to the station doors. The cowboy sat outside in a small, wide white bus with gigantic wheels. Alvin ran out and immediately lost his breath. The cold was like running into an ice wall. The bus driver opened the door and gestured emphatically for him to jump on. He doubled over and climbed onto the bus. The doors shut behind him instantly.

Alvin sat beside the cowboy and looked around the empty bus. He couldn't believe he had actually chosen to go out in this cold again. But the heat of the bus already warmed his cheeks. "Thanks," he said to the cowboy. "Thanks for paying for me."

The cowboy threw his cigarette butt on the bus floor. He didn't stamp it out. Alvin did. "I didn't pay nothing extra for you," said the cowboy. "I just told the guy you were coming and that's that. Let's go now," he said loudly to the driver.

The bus rolled slowly down a plowed narrow road, past a video store, a grocery, a bank, a bar. All the windows had shutters over them, so Alvin couldn't see any lights inside. Now there were small, brightly colored wood houses and then metal shacks that seemed like oversized boxes. He wondered if the map on the web was wrong and there were roads all through Canada, after all. But within minutes the road ended and the bus crunched its way across snow. Everything was white for as far as he could see through the weak light of midday. Everything was flat. Everything was empty.

They drove in silence for a long time. So much nothingness.

The driver slid to a stop. "Twenty meters ahead."

"Now, that's something," said the cowboy. "Incredible."

A huge polar bear stood there. Its sides caved in, but its hind part was expansive and powerful. Its fur seemed yellow against the white ground. The bus motor hummed; black smoke poured out the exhaust pipe and hung in the air. The polar bear didn't turn to look at the bus. It stood immobile, nose lifted at the seemingly endless snow.

The jab of fear Alvin had felt at first sight of the bear dulled. This was a quiet beast. Almost serene. The snow was his natural environment, his home. The three of them, Alvin thought, were the intruders. The bear allowed them to watch, but he wasn't going to allow them to bother him. He was in charge. He surveyed the unending white horizon like a king. Awe filled Alvin.

"What's going on?" said the cowboy. "What's the matter with that bear?"

The driver turned in his seat and fixed his black eyes on the cowboy. His nose and lips were different from Manitok's, but his eyes were the same. Alvin decided he liked Inuk eyes. They were like deep holes. "Polar bears are patient. They stand four, five, six hours. Longer. The Inuit mimic the bear."

"Why's he patient?" said Alvin. "What's he waiting for?"

"The animals of the winter are white. Could you spot a white animal in snow?"

Alvin shook his head.

"So?" said the cowboy.

"So the polar bear stands still and the animals don't see him. And they move. When they move, the polar bear sees them. Then he runs." The driver paused. "He runs fast." The driver's eyes shone bright as he stared at the cowboy. "And he crushes them with one blow." The driver sat up straight and turned his back on Alvin and the cowboy. When he spoke again, he directed his words at the polar bear up ahead. "He even kills people."

A lump formed in Alvin's throat.

"Polar bears will go right into an igloo to attack a person. Only the dogs keep them away."

"Why isn't he interested in us?" asked the cowboy.

"Buses don't taste good."

Alvin laughed in relief.

The driver turned his head and looked at Alvin. He laughed too.

Only the cowboy wasn't laughing. He should

lighten up. Alvin jabbed him in the ribs in a friendly way.

The cowboy made a short, dry cough. "He doesn't look too good at hunting. He's skinny."

"He's young," said the driver. "Older bears steal his food."

The cowboy tapped his heel on the floor as though he was suddenly antsy to get up and move around. "Is that all the bear's going to do?"

"Probably," said the driver. "The noise of the bus scares the animals he's hunting. Nothing will move as long as we're here."

"Then let's go back," said the cowboy.

The driver made a big loop on the snow and those giant wheels crunched back toward town. It took a long time. When they were finally near the first set of shacks, the cowboy pointed. "Isn't that a bear?"

This polar bear was smaller and skinnier. Its fur seemed to hang off its bones. It crouched by an open garbage dump. The driver stopped the bus and pulled out a rifle from beside his seat. He opened the doors and held the rifle ready. Cold air filled the bus instantly. The driver stepped down onto the snow and took aim. He was a small man, shorter even than Manitok. And a lot thinner. The bear was bigger than him by far. But with that gun, the driver was the predator.

Alvin stared in horror. It didn't seem right to kill the bear just for rummaging in the garbage. Besides, this bear looked like he was starving. Alvin stood up and ran to the door of the bus, ready to protest.

The crack of the rifle shocked him.

The bear jumped to all fours. Then he looked at the driver. The driver shot again. And the bear stood there. The driver shot once more. The bear ran.

Toward the bus.

The driver jumped on, pushing Alvin aside. He dropped his rifle on the floor and got in his seat. He pushed the button by his seat and the door closed. Alvin sat on the floor of the bus where the driver had knocked him and looked at the huge bear running straight for him. He jumped up and screamed at the very moment the bear slammed into the door. The bus rocked, and Alvin was knocked to the floor again. The driver gunned the engine and drove ahead.

"I'll kill him." The cowboy grabbed the rifle off the floor. He aimed it at the bear through the window.

"Blanks," said the driver. "Don't shoot. The Plexiglas is reinforced, but the window still might break."

"Blanks? What good are blanks against a polar bear?"

"Against this one, no good. But most of them run away. This is a rogue bear. He needs to go to polar bear jail."

Alvin climbed onto a seat and looked out the window. The bear trotted behind them. "Polar bear jail," he said, clutching the edge of the seat. "What's that?"

The driver looked over his shoulder. He didn't increase the speed of the bus, though. "A helicopter drops a dome of bars over the rogue bears. It's like an oval jail. Then they tranquilize the bears and the helicopter takes them far off, out onto the tundra. Sometimes they never come back." The driver looked over his shoulder again. "He's turned around, heading back to his garbage heap. Martin will have to go after him."

"You mean Manitok?" asked Alvin.

"Yes." The driver looked at Alvin and smiled.

Alvin watched the bear retreat. He should have felt relief—for the fact that the bear hadn't crushed him and for the fact that the driver hadn't shot the bear. He should have cheered. But he couldn't move. His whole body felt limp, drained of energy from that scare, as if he was nothing more than a puddle of water turning quickly to ice.

CHAPTER SIXTEEN

Fox

The driver ran inside the station. Alvin and the cowboy doubled over against the cold and followed. As they came through the door, the driver rushed past them out to the bus again.

Manitok handed Alvin a sandwich. "I bought peanut butter at the Hudson Bay company store. American kids love it, right?"

"Thanks," said Alvin.

"Eating alone isn't good. I've got to gather helpers to catch that rogue bear. If you want to wait, I'll eat my sandwich with you when I get back."

"I'm used to eating alone," said Alvin. He ate

breakfast alone almost every day. "And I'm really hungry."

"All right. Sit on the bench and stay put."

Alvin sat beside the cowboy.

"There's nowhere you can go anyway," said Manitok. "You'd freeze in your clothes." He went into his office and came out dressed in the parka and breeches and those big boots. He saw Alvin looking at them. *"Kamiks,"* he said. "They're made of sealskin, lined with a sock of dog skin."

"Dog?" said Alvin. "Real dog?"

"Most *kamiks* are lined with caribou or seal. But dog's the best you can get." Manitok ran outside to the waiting bus.

Alvin lifted his sandwich to his mouth. The cowboy watched. Alvin hesitated. "Hey, man," he said, "I didn't eat all day yesterday."

The cowboy looked away. "Steve is late." He glanced at Alvin, then quickly looked away again. "Go on and eat."

Alvin took a bite. The cowboy kept looking away. "Okay, okay." He ripped the sandwich in half. "Here."

The cowboy grinned and wolfed down his half. "I'll buy you a drink, buddy." He got up and stood in front of the hot beverage machine. "Chicken broth, hot chocolate, hot Coke—"

Alvin laughed. "They don't have hot Coke."

"Sure they do," said the cowboy. "They have all sorts of wonders. Listen to this: melted polar bear turds—"

"I'll take the hot chocolate," Alvin said.

They drank hot chocolate. Then they drank chicken broth. Then they drank more hot chocolate. "Where is that guy?" said the cowboy. The clock ticked past two. Past two thirty.

Alvin remembered the bag of pretzels. He dug it out of his pack and they shared that.

It was now two forty-five.

The door burst open and a man as tall as the cowboy stomped his *kamiks* in the center of the floor.

"You're late, Steve," said the cowboy.

Steve pulled back his hood and long, black hair streaked with gray came out over the fur edging. He was an Inuk, like Manitok and the bus driver. So some of them did grow taller than five feet, after all. Steve carried a bunch of pelts over his shoulder, all roped together. He flopped them onto the floor in front of the cowboy.

"I hate it when people are late," said the cowboy.

"I do not have a watch," said Steve stiffly. He had a heavy accent.

"Buy one," said the cowboy.

Steve shrugged. "Things happen when they happen."

"You said that last time. And last time I told you I hate it when people are late."

"These foxes are good." Steve tapped the furs with the toe of his *kamik*.

The cowboy got on his knees and examined the pelts.

Steve stared at Alvin as though he'd just noticed him.

Alvin stared back. "What's your name? Your real one, I mean."

"My birth name is Inukjuak," said Steve proudly. "But the Anglican missionary christened me Stephen. White people call me Steve for short."

"I'm not white," said Alvin.

"I can see that," said Steve. "You are the first black person I have ever seen that is not on a TV or movie screen."

"Ever heard of Matthew Henson?"

"No. Is that your name?"

Alvin shook his head. "So what should I call you?"

"I do not know," said Steve.

"I'll call you Fox," said Alvin. It sounded childish

the instant Alvin said it, as though he was six or something. He wanted to snatch the words back out of the air.

But Fox said, "I like that. Fox is a good name for a trapper. The next time I meet a black person, I will introduce myself as Fox."

"If you two are through being buddies," said the cowboy, "we can talk money."

While the cowboy and Fox talked, Alvin touched the furs. They were exquisitely soft. He wanted to crawl into the middle of the pile.

Then the cowboy slung the pelts over his shoulder and headed for the door.

"You leaving?" Alvin asked quickly.

"I'm going to the hotel. The Arctic Inn. It's more like a creaking barn. But it's home for one more night. See you later, buddy." He left.

Fox looked surprised that Alvin was staying behind, but he didn't say anything.

For an instant Alvin had the urge to run after the cowboy—the only other American around. If he'd thought fast enough, he could have sent a letter home to Mamma and Grandma with the cowboy. Who knew when he'd get a chance like that again?

He turned to Fox. He better not blow this chance

anyway. "Manitok said you're from Baffin Island. From Pang-something."

"Pangnirtung."

"How far north is that?" Alvin asked.

Fox turned around and went out the door.

What had happened? Alvin sank onto the bench.

Fox came back inside. He sat beside Alvin and opened a map. He pointed to a spot in the southeast of Baffin Island, a little ways south of the Arctic Circle. "Pangnirtung," he said. "The bishop of the Arctic visits there."

All Alvin knew about bishops was that they were part of some churches that he wasn't a member of. "Oh."

Fox swept his hand across the map. "The whole Arctic. He goes everywhere. He gathers souls."

Everywhere. That bishop goes everywhere. Alvin licked his lips. This was really it—the way to make it all happen. "Can I go with you to Pangnirtung?"

Fox looked dumbstruck. "You want to come with me?"

"I need to see the bishop of the Arctic." Alvin breathed hard. Fox waited with unwavering eyes. Alvin shook his head. "I want to go to the Arctic with him." Fox still didn't speak. "It's because my mother,

my family . . . because . . . " If he couldn't get
Hardette to understand, there was no way he'd get
Fox to. "I'm not good at explaining it."

"I do not ask for an explanation. *Piusiunngituk.* That
is not my way."

Gratitude washed over Alvin. He would love being
with the Inuit, just like Matthew Henson did. "How
much will it cost?"

"I did not agree to take you," said Fox. He crossed
his arms over his chest and tucked his hands in his
armpits. "I said only that I do not ask an explanation. You are young."

"Not as young as you think. And I've traveled far
by myself already," said Alvin.

"I can see that. Is it legal?"

"By whose laws?" said Alvin. "What do Inuit people
say?"

"I killed my first polar bear when I was twelve,"
said Fox. "I was still not a man, but after that, things
were different."

"I'm twelve," said Alvin.

Fox fell silent.

"I have to keep going." Alvin's voice was thin with
need. "I have to."

"Family," Fox said at last, "family is the center."

He let his hands drop. "The bishop should come to Pangnirtung soon. You can stay with me till he comes."

Alvin let out his breath. "Thank you. Thank you so much. So what will you charge me?"

"Young people do not have much money." Fox looked him up and down. "And you do not weigh a lot. You will not use much petrol. If you help me load the plane, I will take you free."

"I'll load everything. Everything. Thank you." Alvin jumped to his feet. "Let's go."

"Tomorrow," said Fox.

"What time?"

Fox laughed. "You are like the man in the leather boots. Always asking about time. What time do you want?"

"How's seven? Can we go at seven?"

"Seven," said Fox. "Seven it is."

Alvin remembered the cowboy lamenting about how late Fox came. "Does that mean you'll show up at eight?"

"That means I will show up," said Fox. He folded his map and walked toward the door.

"Fox?"

Fox turned around.

"Will you see Manitok again before you go?"

"I do not know."

"Please, if you see him, don't tell him that I'm going with you to Pangnirtung."

Fox looked at Alvin with calm eyes.

"He'd get angry," said Alvin.

"No. He would not get angry."

How could Fox know that? "Please. You shouldn't be the one to tell him." Alvin didn't add that no one should tell him.

Fox waited. Finally he said, "You are old enough to choose where you go. And if you choose badly, the bishop can advise you."

"But what about now? What about Manitok?"

"I will unload, then I will shop. I will not say things I do not have to say."

"Unload?" said Alvin. "I thought the fox skins were all you had with you. I'll help you unload."

"I carry feathers. And I do not need help with them."

Feathers? But before Alvin could ask further, Fox had left.

The rest of the day passed so slowly, Alvin thought he'd lose his mind. Manitok was nice to him, but he kept calling him Pete. It made Alvin feel disoriented every time. Manitok was on and off the phone and the computer, working out all the arrangements for Alvin to go south on the next train, which would leave Sunday afternoon. The Royal Canadian Mounted Police would be waiting for him in Winnipeg.

Around four o'clock, Manitok put on his parka and breeches, picked up Alvin's jacket, and left the station. He said he'd be gone only an hour or so. When he came back, he carried Alvin's jacket but also a big plastic garbage bag. He pulled out winter clothing: huge mittens and *kamiks* and a parka and breeches just like his. He told Alvin they were his old stuff and said it was lucky Alvin was so tall for his age. Alvin almost laughed at that. Manitok had no idea how tall the kids in Alvin's town were.

Manitok said Alvin should put the clothes on and they'd go to his place for the night. His mother and aunt and cousins all wanted to meet him. They had seen him asleep—but they wanted to know him awake.

Alvin couldn't risk not being at the station when Fox showed up. He refused to go.

Manitok sat beside him and said it would be more comfortable at his house. It would be warmer. Dinner would be hot.

Alvin was steadfast.

Manitok never got angry through this. Mamma would have put her hands on her hips in frustration. She would have paced and raised her voice. But this man spoke without impatience, always respectful. Maybe Fox was right and Manitok wouldn't get angry if he explained what he wanted to do. But it didn't matter really, because there was a big difference between not getting angry and agreeing. Manitok was in charge of Alvin in some official way now; he'd never let him leave with Fox.

Manitok put the clothes back in the garbage bag and stuck it in the corner. He took off his own outer clothes and made them peanut butter sandwiches for dinner. He seemed to think Alvin would be delighted. The funny thing was, Alvin didn't care that much for peanut butter, but it was clear Manitok thought it was a great treat.

After dinner Manitok put on his outer clothes again and said he'd be back faster this time. He took Alvin's jacket. Then, after a moment's thought, he took one of the old *kamiks* out of the garbage bag, too. He was smart.

Manitok returned carrying a folded cot. He set it up beside the sofa and lay down to sleep.

Alvin stared at him in dismay. He had hoped that

Fox would come early enough in the morning that they'd be gone before Manitok came to the station. Now everything was ruined.

He stretched out on the sofa, with the pillow and blanket, and worry gave way to guilt: Manitok had no covers or pillow. When he sat up to tell Manitok he'd take the cot instead, Manitok was already asleep.

Alvin lay back and closed his eyes. He told himself that it would work out—he'd think better in the morning, after a good night's sleep; He'd find a way to leave with Fox without Manitok stopping them. But sleep wouldn't come. It seemed like hours and hours. Finally he got up and went into the main room to check the clock. He couldn't count on sunlight to wake him, because Manitok had told him that in January the sun shone for only a few hours right in the middle of the day. It would still be dark when Fox came.

He turned on the light. Eleven P.M. He shut the light and went back into the office.

Manitok was sitting up on his cot. He took Alvin's jacket off the back of the door, where it hung beside his own parka and breeches, and balled it up as a pillow under his head on the cot. "Put your shoes on next time," he mumbled, and fell asleep.

It was good advice; Alvin's feet were chilled. He tried again to sleep. Nothing. When he felt sure it was morning, he got up. He put on his shoes, and this time he carried his notebook with him into the main room. He turned on the light; 2:40 A.M. He opened the notebook to the Xerox of Matthew Henson's grave, which Manitok had put right back where he'd taken it from, as Alvin knew he would have. He looked at the inscription on the gravestone, the words he'd memorized:

THE LURE OF THE ARCTIC IS TUGGING AT MY HEART. TO ME THE TRAIL IS CALLING! THE OLD TRAIL—THE TRAIL THAT IS ALWAYS NEW.

He folded the paper and stuck it inside his shirt, against his skin, and shut the light.

Manitok was sitting up again when Alvin came back into the office, but he didn't say anything this time.

The same thing happened the next two times Alvin got up to check the clock.

By the fifth time, it was six o'clock. He gave up on sleep, sat on the bench in the main room, and waited.

Manitok came out of the office after eight, looking as bleary-eyed as Alvin felt. He used the bathroom. Then he put on his outer clothes and left, saying he'd return soon. He didn't even take Alvin's jacket.

This was it; the chance he'd been hoping for. Fox should come now. Right now. Alvin jogged around the perimeter of the main room, to keep from thinking too much.

A little before nine Manitok came back with a Tupperware container. It turned out to hold salted trout, which smelled funny.

They ate breakfast together, side by side on the office sofa, slow and quiet, as though they'd been friends for years. Alvin didn't try the fish, and Manitok didn't insist, wolfing it down. He ate a peanut butter sandwich and wondered now if Manitok had acted like it was a treat yesterday just to be polite.

Something about that sandwich undid Alvin: The long night caught up with him. He was weary. He yawned. And he was discouraged. Maybe Fox wouldn't come at all. But even if he did, Manitok was in the station again. He stood up. "I need exercise," he said.

Manitok just nodded.

Alvin jogged again. It was nine thirty and there

was no sign of Fox. He used the bathroom and looked out the window. Nothing moved. The whole town seemed to be asleep. Maybe no one got up early on a Sunday morning. Maybe even church waited till that little period of midday light to hold service.

He checked back in the office. Manitok sat on the sofa, snoring, with Alvin's jacket balled behind his neck and the blanket tucked around his shoulders.

What could he do without a jacket?

But the jacket wasn't warm enough anyway, that's what Manitok had said.

And there was something better than his jacket in this office.

He quietly took his backpack and put it out in the main room. Then, without letting himself think twice, he went back into Manitok's office and took the garbage bag from the corner. He opened it in the main room and pulled out the old parka and breeches and mittens and one *kamik*. The second *kamik* was missing. When Manitok took it away last night, he hadn't brought it back. Well, okay, his sneakers would just have to do.

Alvin went to shut the office door. That's when he saw Manitok's new *kamiks* sitting on the floor. Just sitting there. Waiting.

Manitok had another pair of *kamiks*—even though one of them was at home—old but functional. Alvin knew what he had to do. Before he could talk himself out of it, he grabbed the *kamiks* and shut the door.

He stood in the main room. His pulse was loud inside his head. How could he take Manitok's *kamiks*, especially after Manitok had been so good to him?

But Manitok said himself that Alvin would never survive without proper clothing. Manitok would understand.

Alvin put on all his sweatshirts plus his sweatpants and got into the parka and breeches. There were no zippers or snaps—the clothes just pulled on. The outfit was roomy around the middle even with three sweatshirts on, and he had to bunch up the sleeves and legs like accordians, because Manitok was taller than him, but these clothes would make the rest of the journey possible. He shoved his sneakers into his backpack and put on the *kamiks*.

This was a lousy thing to do.

The memory of the savage cold in the freight car came back.

Alvin took the money from his backpack. How much could a pair of *kamiks* cost? He had no idea.

There was more than three hundred dollars in his hands. That had to last him as far as he was going, with enough left for the journey home.

He counted out fifty dollars. That must be enough. Besides, now he remembered reading that the Inuit didn't even use money. They simply worked and traded for whatever they needed. That's where the Inuit had everyone beat. Surely Manitok could get himself a new pair of *kamiks* with these fifty dollars if he also worked and traded.

It wasn't fair that Manitok would have to work and trade because Alvin had taken his *kamiks*. But what choice did Alvin have?

He walked over to the desk. The breeches made little swishing sounds as his legs rubbed against each other. Manitok didn't move, though.

Alvin left the money by the computer keyboard. He took a piece of paper and wrote, "Thank you." He went out into the main room and paced.

It didn't feel right. Even fancy sneakers cost more than fifty dollars. *Kamiks* had to cost a lot. He went back into Manitok's office one last time. Manitok slept soundly, with his mouth open. Alvin put another fifty dollars on the pile of money. He stared at it. Then he added twenty more. He weighted all the money down with the can of tuna fish.

He backed out of the room and shut the door softly. As he turned around, he jumped. Fox stood behind him. What had he seen? Alvin put his finger to his lips in the hush sign. Fox nodded. They left silently.

Fox's airplane was small, with huge skis for landing on snow. While they loaded big burlap bags into the area behind the two front seats, he told Alvin that in the summer the skis were replaced with pontoons for landing on water. He described lots of things about the plane, shouting above the engine roar. Alvin was only half listening as he climbed in and shut the door. All he wanted was to get away before Manitok woke.

The motor made the whole plane vibrate. Alvin was in a plane, a real plane, for the first time in his life. Inside his head he'd been praying they'd take off fast. But now he changed his mind. This plane felt flimsy, as though it might come apart in midair. He turned to Fox in an instant of panic.

Fox reached across him, grabbed the seat belt, and buckled him in. He put a pair of earplugs on Alvin's lap. Then he buckled himself in and adjusted the controls.

Alvin put in the earplugs. The sound of the motor came through, but dull now. He searched for something to hold on to. There were no armrests. He reached his left hand over his left shoulder and gripped the back of his seat. He reached the other hand between his legs and gripped the lower front rim of his seat.

The takeoff was smooth, like sliding into water, only up instead of down. They were really in the air. The motor noise dulled even more, to a loud hum that gently massaged them. Alvin let his mittened hands rest in his lap and, gradually, gradually, he almost relaxed. But then he looked out the passenger window into black air. His stomach lurched. The plane felt so thin and fragile, he had the sensation that if he leaned too far, it would tilt. He looked across Fox out the other window. He had the same sensation. The inside of this plane was no bigger than a car. A small car. Now Alvin clutched the lower rim of his seat with both hands and looked straight ahead, his body rigid.

The air warmed a little. Alvin pushed back his hood. He smelled a mixture of machine oil and something familiar that seemed to come from the bags they had loaded. Outside they hadn't smelled at all, but now he could catch their scent. He twisted around in his seat and sniffed hard.

"Grain," shouted Fox, loud enough that Alvin just caught the word. Then he said something else about the general store. He'd gone shopping in Churchill.

Alvin breathed in the dry, slightly sweet smell and tried to let go of the tension in his back. He was aware of exhaustion lurking at the edges of his consiousness. He fought it off.

The ride took hours and hours. Alvin kept expecting sunlight, and even though he was afraid, he wanted to see the world from a plane's view. But sunlight never came. Fox shouted things now and then. He explained that in Pangnirtung the sun didn't shine from November through February. He said there was a kind of hazy daylight—not sun, just light—from about nine or ten in the morning to about two or three in the afternoon. But the trip was so long, they'd arrive after daylight had ended.

Alvin hadn't asked about light. He didn't ask anything. Fox shouted on his own, and sometimes he just happened to talk about what was on Alvin's mind.

At one point Fox touched Alvin's knee. "Manitok's old clothes."

Alvin tensed up for a confrontation.

But Fox only smiled. "Manitok did good to make you that gift. He told me he likes you, Pete."

Alvin burned with shame. He wished he could tuck his feet under him so Fox wouldn't realize the *kamiks* were Manitok's new ones. He prayed there would be a wonderful sale on snow gear in Churchill.

After a while, Fox stopped shouting even those few words. They passed the rest of the trip in silence, with Alvin drifting in and out of sleep.

Eventually Alvin saw a red beacon below and they landed, with a terrifying smack and a slide through frozen, starry space. Down here on the ground, the air wasn't black anymore—it was gray, over blue snow.

Fox took out his earplugs and put them in a little well between the seats. Alvin popped out his and dropped them on top of Fox's. Fox reached across Alvin and opened his door. The icy air slammed Alvin in the face. They each pulled up their hood and jumped out their own door.

The propellers had stopped—the motor was off but the roaring sound continued. Alvin turned around and almost got swept off his feet by the wind. That roar was the howl of wind over snow.

Fox came around the back of the plane, closed the door behind Alvin, and walked quickly. There were small homes ahead and a church spire shot up into the stars.

Oh, the stars. They surrounded them, so many and so bright that Alvin felt he could reach out and touch them. He couldn't look at them for long, though, because the cold on his face shocked him into motion. The air in the plane had been almost warm, but now he recognized that he was significantly more north—in a significantly colder climate.

Alvin tucked his head against the wind and followed close behind Fox. They must have walked for more than fifteen minutes before they went inside a house.

There was only one person in the room, a thin, tall white man in ordinary pants and a turtleneck shirt. He got up from a chair and came to them. "Stephen, welcome home. So this is the runaway." His accent was slight, and different from Fox's. It was unlike any Alvin had ever heard.

At the word "runaway," Alvin stiffened.

Fox took off his hood. His face carried surprise. "This is Pete, who has a family problem. He needs to see the bishop of the Arctic."

Alvin pushed back his hood and started to pull off his parka over his head.

The man held his hand up in the halt signal. "I'll handle it from here. Keep your parka on, young man. We're going to my place." He pulled on a parka, breeches, and boots and pushed Alvin ahead of him out the door.

CHAPTER SEVENTEEN

The Missionary

They tramped through the snow with the man pulling Alvin this way and that, to another house. Once inside, the man took off his outer clothes and boots. He cocked his head at Alvin. "Wouldn't you be more comfortable without all those extra clothes on?"

Alvin took off his gear and made a little stack of it on the floor, which was dank and cold.

The man pulled a chair over and offered it to him.

"Sir, are you the bishop of the Arctic, sir?"

"No." The man smiled. "I'm only an ordinary Anglican missionary. My name is Donald. Have a seat, won't you, Peter?"

Alvin sat in the chair and perched his feet on his backpack to keep them warm. The missionary sat in another chair and waited. Alvin cleared his throat. "I need to see the bishop."

"Why?"

"I want to travel with him."

The missionary made a little click of his tongue. "The bishop doesn't live here, you know. He only visits."

"I know. But he's visiting soon."

"Did Stephen tell you that? You can't take an Inuk's word on time. They have no sense of it."

There was condescension in this missionary's voice. Alvin took an immediate dislike to him.

"So, where do you want to travel to?"

"Ellesmere Island."

The missionary thought about that. "Stephen said you have a problem."

"That's my problem. Can you help me get there?"

The missionary pursed his lips. "Wait here." He left.

The room had a stove near one wall with a big pot on it and a table and three chairs beside it. Alvin's chair matched the other three chairs. There were shelves with dishes and pots. A big, old sofa pressed against another wall. The bookshelf near it was packed full. In front of the sofa was a low table with a partially done jigsaw puzzle. Pushed against the walls here and there were boxes and small packing crates. There were three windows; all had closed shutters.

Two doors led off this room. The missionary had gone through one. And now a girl maybe six years old, an Inuk, peeked out the other. When Alvin looked at her, she shut the door. The door opened again and a second girl, slightly older, peeked at him and smiled. The little girl peeked out beneath her, then they both disappeared behind the shut door.

The missionary came back in. "Peter," he said, "Peter, you've given me a tall order."

It was strange enough being called Pete all the time, and now Alvin had to get used to Peter.

"All right, Peter." The missionary sighed. "Let's think this through. Let's be rational." He sighed again. "Can you tell me why you want to go to Ellesmere Island?"

Alvin knew immediately that his answer wouldn't qualify as rational in this missionary's eyes. "I can't say."

The missionary gave a loud wheeze. "No one travels

north in January. In summer there's a boat to Nanisivik, on the Borden Peninsula." He looked at Alvin. "It's at the northern tip of Baffin Island. From there another boat goes to Grise Fiord."

Alvin perked up. Grise Fiord was near the research base of Alert or Eureka—he remembered that from reading on the web. Maybe someone at one of the research bases would help him. "I want to go to Eureka," he said.

The missionary's blue eyes went sharp. He pulled a chair over from the table and sat facing Alvin. "Now we're making progress. Is someone at Eureka expecting you?"

Alvin shook his head.

The missionary folded his hands in his lap and crossed his legs at the ankle. "The research bases don't allow visitors. Why do you want to go to Eureka?"

Alvin shrugged. "Ellesmere Island is the northern-most land in the world."

"Actually," said the missionary, lifting his chin, "parts of Greenland are more northern." With his chin up like that, he made Alvin think of Hardette. "I'm from Greenland, you see. However, Ellesmere Island is the farthest north in Canada. It's only one thousand kilometers from Eureka to the North Pole."

"What's that in miles?" said Alvin.

"Ah, yes, you're American. Let's see, that's a little more than six hundred miles." The missionary rubbed his knee through his pants. "One thousand kilometers of frozen ocean. You can't begin to imagine how cold it is that far north." The missionary looked beyond Alvin at the wall. "Storms are common up there. The winds blow so hard that you can't move at all. Do you know how many people have frozen to death in the Arctic?"

"No one could know that," said Alvin.

"A lot," said the missionary, ignoring Alvin.

Alvin saw what the missionary was doing—trying to wear him down, trying to frighten him.

"You couldn't stay warm," said the missionary. "Even in the clothes you stole from the Churchill stationmaster."

Alvin tapped his feet on his backpack. So Manitok and the missionary had already talked. That's why the missionary was waiting for him in Fox's house. Of course. He'd been ambushed.

What else did this missionary know? Alvin didn't like his phony calm voice and the way he thought he could make Alvin feel silly and small.

"And, by the way, did you know that a good pair of *kamiks* alone cost nearly two hundred American dollars? *Kamiks* like those aren't sold in stores. They're handmade. It's lucky that stationmaster has an extra pair. Ah, Peter. The Arctic is harsh. If you wandered outside the research base and got lost . . . "

"I have a compass," said Alvin. He dug into his backpack.

"A compass won't help, of course," said the missionary, looking around the room as though Alvin was of little interest, "since, as you well know, the North Magnetic Pole is not identical to the North Pole. No, indeed. The North Magnetic Pole is south of Ellesmere Island, on Bathurst Island. So compasses give you wrong information when you're that far north."

Alvin hadn't heard about two north poles before. And the missionary probably guessed that. He was playing a terrible game—trying to make Alvin think he didn't know anything, trying to make him turn himself over to the great white man who knew everything. "I could find my way using the stars." That's what the Inuit traditionally did. He had read that.

The missionary finally looked directly at Alvin. "Hitch your wagon to a star, is that it?"

What did that mean? Alvin looked back in silence.

"Where's your home, Peter?"

Alvin tapped his feet again.

"What's the real reason you want to go to Ellesmere Island?"

"You ask the same question over and over. My grandma would call you stubborn."

The missionary smiled. "Is that what she calls you?"

Alvin opened his mouth to respond, but he yawned.

"Do you realize how extremely lucky you've been to get this far without something dreadful happening? The world is full of dangers, Peter. Dangerous things. Dangerous people."

"You sound like my mother." Alvin yawned again.

The missionary smiled. "When's the last time you ate?"

"I had breakfast."

"Let's eat. Then we can figure a way to get you back home."

"I'm not going home," said Alvin.

"Yes, you are, young man. It's the best place for you, I can tell you that." There was a sadness in his voice that touched Alvin.

"You don't know," Alvin said quietly.

"Then tell me. Are you running away from something or running to something? Which is it, Peter?"

Alvin sat silent.

The missionary put his fingertips together and watched Alvin for several minutes. Then he stood up. "For now you can stay here. You can sleep on the couch. We can talk. There's all the time in the world to talk here." He took a can of carrots out of a box on the floor. "We can add carrots to the fish stew as a treat. What do you say to that?"

"Thank you," mumbled Alvin, though he knew it didn't matter what he said about anything. This missionary thought he knew everything.

Maybe that's why he was so obviously lonely; no one likes someone like that. Maybe this missionary never really heard or helped anyone.

CHAPTER EIGHTEEN

Seagulls

As soon as the missionary finally went into another room, Alvin pulled on all his gear fast, and left.

The first thing he saw when he opened his eyes against the sting of the cold was the deep orange moon. It was just a sliver. And it was surrounded by zillions of stars. When Alvin had landed in the plane with Fox, he'd had the impression of stars everywhere. But Fox had trudged so quickly over the snow and Alvin had had to work so hard to keep up with him, fighting the force of the wind, that Alvin hadn't had a chance to really look around. Now that the

wind had slowed to a constant whistle, he looked
everywhere. The vast sky enveloped him. He was like
a dot on a piece of black construction paper and
someone had sprinkled the whole paper with silver
flecks. Everything was dark black and silver, except
for the moon—that claw-sharp, orange moon. It was
as beautiful as anything Alvin had ever imagined.

Alvin shuffled down the path they'd taken earlier,
the snow squeaking loudly under his *kamiks*. He was
heading back toward Fox's house. He trusted Fox.
Donald had been waiting in Fox's house because he
knew Fox wouldn't bring him to the missionary. Fox
knew better than that—anyone would know better
than that. Anyone would know the missionary was
the sort of person to just send him right back. So
Fox must have had another plan for helping Alvin.

Fox had killed his first polar bear when he was
twelve. He got it; he got why Alvin was on this trip.

A dog barked. Others joined in. And now they
were growling fiercely. It sounded like dozens of
them. Alvin ran and fell. He could feel them tearing
at his feet. He scrambled up. The dogs weren't on
him. They must have been tied. And now he saw
them—tangled together and climbing over one
another. Someone came out of a house and shouted

to the dogs. They quieted down instantly. The person turned to Alvin, hesitated a moment, then went back into the house.

Matthew Henson had actually learned to drive that kind of dog.

Alvin felt sick for a moment. It was almost as though he was living Henson's life. Nothing scared Henson.

But Alvin wasn't Henson, and the thought of what might lay ahead brought that powerful sickening feeling.

He couldn't give in to it. Not now. Definitely not now, out here in the cold.

He shuffled faster. He pulled down the fur-edged hood so that it half covered his eyes. Was this the way he'd come with the missionary? The houses were close together, and they all looked the same. He passed an open garbage heap and thought of the rogue polar bear in Churchill. He remembered it chasing the bus.

In a burst of clarity he realized this was insane. If he didn't freeze, a polar bear would eat him. He turned to go to the last house he'd passed when a white cloud of noise descended around him.

Terrified, he stumbled backward and fell again.

Gulls crowded together on the snow, screaming. A huge one hopped close to his head. He swung his arm. The bird fluttered, then landed on his stomach. Its head pointed into the wind, but its eye looked right at Alvin.

He got to his knees and crawled to keep the birds off his face. But he wasn't sure he was crawling in the right direction. The gulls had obliterated his footprints. What if he was heading out toward sea? What if the snow beneath him turned to slush? He stopped crawling. If he stood up and turned around slowly, he'd be able to see a house. He'd go to the first one he saw.

Alvin started to get up. That's when he felt the grip on his elbow. He screamed.

"*Asorssuak*," said a woman's voice. "*Ajungilak ajungilak asorssuak.*"

Alvin threw himself into the Inuk's arms.

"*Oonh-he,*" she said.

Alvin grabbed her tight and they shuffled together. The cold bore a glittering, frozen hole down through his nostrils clear to his stomach.

They shuffled past the dogs, which growled low. Alvin didn't dare look. He felt that if he moved his eyes too fast, they'd shatter, like thin glass.

The woman opened a door and the snow around Alvin lit up. She pushed him inside. At last he was breathing warm air again.

The room was about the size of the missionary's room, only there weren't any other doors. Two girls stood in dirty dresses with fur *kamiks*. They were younger than the girls he'd seen at the missionary's house. A man in jeans and a plaid shirt smiled at him. His face had deep lines; his hair was long like Fox's. The woman took off her parka, and her black hair cascaded down even longer than his. She pulled off her *kamiks* and stiff breeches. Underneath she had on a rumpled dress. Then she climbed back into her *kamiks*. She gestured to Alvin to take off his outer clothes. He wanted to move, but his body didn't have the energy. The woman gently pushed back his hood. Then she stood waiting. He finally took off his *kamiks* and got out of the parka and breeches. The cold of the floor penetrated his socks. He put his *kamiks* back on.

There was a couch, four chairs at a dining table, bedding on the floor in a corner. In another corner was a toilet that didn't have a flush handle. A chemical toilet. An electric lamp stood beside a smaller table that held a sewing machine. Beside it on the floor was a small television. One wall was covered with gull wings, fanned out and sewn together as decoration. A bird with wings like those had hopped on Alvin's stomach only moments before. He shuddered.

The smell of kerosene permeated everything. He recognized it because of Alicia, a girl in his school; her mother had used kerosene to kill the lice in her hair last year. No other smell was like that. It came from a stove in the center of the room.

The woman smiled. "Aima," she said, pointing to herself. "Oodlateeta," she said, pointing to the man.

Alvin smiled back. He felt he should do something formal, so he bowed.

The woman laughed. She turned to the little girls and said something. They ran to the toilet and used it, right in front of him. He looked away as soon as he realized what they were doing.

The bigger of the two girls walked over and took a close look at Alvin. She picked her nose. The littler girl walked up beside her and farted and laughed. Alvin had to work to keep back laughter. Why didn't the mother scold them for picking their nose and farting in front of people?

But then he looked around. This was where they lived. One big room. Together all the time. No one had privacy. Things that would be rude back home couldn't be avoided here. He smiled at the girls.

They took their *kamiks* off and snuggled into their bedrolls. The woman patted a bedroll beside the bigger girl. She pointed at Alvin.

Alvin didn't need a second invitation. He looked at the toilet and hesitated. Then he kept his back to everyone and used it. That's what Matthew Henson would have done—he always tried to fit in.

Laughter woke Alvin. Two men were sitting on furs on the floor, leaning toward each other. The one whose face he could see was the man of the house—Oodlateeta. The one whose back was to him had a familiar voice. "Fox?" said Alvin.

Fox turned around. "You napped well. Good. I will talk with you later." He turned back to Oodlateeta and they spoke their language.

The woman, Aima, handed Alvin a cup of hot liquid. He sipped it. Ordinary tea. He drank it slowly. And still the men talked. There was a lazy slowness to everything. So much had changed, and all in just one Sunday. This felt like the longest day of Alvin's life. What time was it anyway? But, then, what did time matter when it was always dark out? He went to his backpack and took out his pennywhistle. He sat on his bedroll and began softly playing "Lazy River."

With the very first note, the men stopped talking. By the time Alvin reached the end of the song, both of the men and Aima and the two little girls, who Aima had promptly woken, sat watching him. He stopped. They waited. Alvin smiled hesitantly. They smiled back. So he played "Mack the Knife."

When he finished, Aima put on her parka and breeches and left. Alvin got worried. He put down his pennywhistle. But Oodlateeta motioned him to play on. So Alvin played "Hello, Dolly!" Then "Mame." Then "Dream a Little Dream of Me." He was glad he'd practiced on the train with Hardette, because now the songs came easily. After each song the men and girls waited for the next.

Aima came in, followed by people, lots of people. Once they'd all taken off their parkas and breeches, Alvin could sort out four more women, six more men, a baby, and five kids. All of them spread furs on the floor and sat looking at Alvin. One of the men took out a pack of cigarettes. Lots of hands stretched out to him, and several people lit up. Smoke filled the room. A bottle passed around among the men, and the sharp smell of whiskey mingled with the smoke. Then the baby passed from one woman to the next, each one sniffing its face hard and long. Two children jumped on each other and fell to the floor, wrestling. Two more joined the fracas. None of the adults paid them any heed.

The two older women wore their hair in low buns. And Aima had her hair twisted up now, too.

The oldest girl produced wads of string. Other children came over and sat with her. They made forms with the strings on their hands. They took the forms from one another, with fingers arranged in intricate ways, and created new forms. The patterns changed with every passing from hand to hand. It was an elaborate game of cat's cradle.

A very old man came over and sat beside Alvin. The adults hushed and watched. Alvin looked around for a cue. What was going on? The old man nodded at him solemnly. Then his eyes went to the pennywhistle. Alvin could sense expectation in everyone.

He picked up the pennywhistle and played "What a Wonderful World." Everyone listened. And waited. The air felt almost ceremonial, like in church sometimes. Slowly he made his way through all the Louis Armstrong songs he knew. Then he worked through Duke Ellington.

The old man finally pointed at the pennywhistle and put his hand out. Alvin set the pennywhistle in his hand. The old man laid it on the floor in front of Alvin's feet.

As though that was a cue, noisy action quickly filled the room. The women talked as they made a meal that sent up exotic smells. The men sat on the floor smoking. The children played their string game or wrestled or did this funny kicking game where one child held out his hand and another child tried to kick it. The highest kicker shouted in triumph. Laughter was frequent. Alvin stayed on his bedroll and watched through the smoky haze. He couldn't understand a word anyone said.

What an odd place this was, how far and different from home. He'd never been this kind of alone before.

A boy came and stood in front of Alvin and sang "Born in the U.S.A." over and over, pretending to strum on a guitar in a bad imitation of Bruce Springsteen.

"Nice," said Alvin. "What else do you sing?"

The boy blinked his eyes. "All the Boss songs," he said with pretty decent English pronunciation. "Do you sing?"

"No," said Alvin.

The boy ran off to the other boys, talking in his own language again.

Alvin caught Fox looking at him. He crawled over there.

Fox spoke before Alvin could say anything. "I cannot take you to Ellesmere Island. It is impossible for my plane to fly that far north at this time of year."

Alvin hadn't mentioned Ellesmere Island to Fox. "That missionary, did he tell you I wanted to go there?"

"Donald sent an e-mail message to the director at Eureka, to see if anyone there knows you. He is waiting for an answer."

E-mail. That's probably how the missionary had found out about Alvin in the first place. It seemed somehow ludicrous that there would be computers so far away from what Alvin thought of as normal life. "Well, I'm going north no matter what. I'll stay with you till the bishop comes, like you said before. I'll stay inside and Donald will never know."

Fox shook his head. "Donald already knows."

"What?" yelped Alvin. "Who told him?"

"He came to my home, looking for you. He planned to go house to house. Pangnirtung has more than twelve hundred people. Many men would have gone out to search. I had to tell him."

Alvin pressed his lips together. "It doesn't matter. He can't stop me."

"Donald says he is in charge of you because he is the one who read the e-mail message about you."

"Why did Manitok write to him?"

"Manitok wrote to many. But it is Sunday. Business computers are off. Donald keeps his computer on always."

"Then it's just an accident that he read it first. He shouldn't be in charge of me. He shouldn't be in charge of anyone."

Fox raised his eyebrows. "You think like an Inuk—we do not give orders."

"That's not what I meant," Alvin admitted, though he wished he didn't have to. "I meant that he isn't the sort of person who should be in charge. He doesn't understand things."

"You do not like him." Fox smiled. "He does not like you, either." He leaned toward Alvin conspiratorily. "He said you must go to him after the meal, but we can eat for many hours."

"That's not enough."

"Donald will try to help you," said Fox. "He is not a bad sort."

"He wants to stop me. That's not going to help

me. Please, Fox, help me really. I have to go
north." Alvin's voice broke. "You killed a polar
bear when you were my age," he whispered. "You
understand."

Fox put his hands on his knees and looked at the
floor. After a while he got up and picked his way over
to the old man. They talked. Oodlateeta and Aima
joined the conversation. Then others were talking,
and everyone was congratulating one another.

The old man looked at Alvin and pointed.
"Kukukulik," he said loudly.

Men here and there nodded. "Kukukulik," they
said, one after another. The children perked up.
"Kukukulik," they said, laughing and pointing at
Alvin. The women looked over from their work.
"Kukukulik," they said.

Alvin got up and went to Fox. "What's going on?"

"It is your Inuk name. Kukukulik. It means 'the
one who plays the flute.'" He laid his hand on Alvin's
shoulder. "The old man Teenaq is right again; your
name matches your nature."

Alvin had been given an Inuk name. What an
amazing thing. "But why? No one here knows me. I
haven't talked to anyone but you."

"Some understand English; they've been listening.

And your music talks. You do not have to go back to Donald."

"You mean that?"

"Oodlateeta and Aima have asked that you stay here in their home. Donald will not object because he has no way to send you back to Churchill until the next plane anyway."

Alvin looked at Oodlateeta, incredulous. "Why are they so generous to me?"

Fox rubbed his hand on Alvin's. "They recently moved. It is their first winter in this home. They say your appearance outside their home was not an accident. Only two days ago Oodlateeta got a walrus. We do not see many walruses in Cumberland Sound these days—this was the first walrus kill in a year." Fox smiled kindly. "Aima comes originally from Greenland, where walrus kills are frequent. It is her favorite meat. They believe the walrus kill was auspicious—a harbinger of your coming, Kukukulik."

Alvin looked around the small room. Four people lived here already. "I'd crowd them," he said.

"Aima said, *'Tupiq qaajjaanngituq.'*" When Fox said the words, everyone within earshot nodded.

"*Tupiq qaajjaanngituq,*" said Aima loudly from her post in front of the stove.

"What's it mean?" asked Alvin.

"In Inuktitut it means 'The tent is not likely to burst.' There's room for you."

Alvin smiled at Aima. "Fox, how do I say 'thank you?'"

"*Qujannamik.*"

"*Qujannamik,*" Alvin said to Aima.

"It is not for long anyway," said Fox. "Teenaq agrees: You are old enough to make this decision. So Oodlateeta has offered to take you to Pond Inlet."

Alvin looked at Oodlateeta, who looked back at him with a triumphantly happy face. He pulled on Fox's hand. "Where's Pond Inlet?"

"At the northern tip of Baffin Island. Far from here. It is the ancestral home of Oodlateeta."

Baffin Island was huge. If Oodlateeta brought him all the way to the northern tip, Alvin would be well on his way to Fort Conger. "Why would he do such a wonderful thing for me?"

"It is not just for you. He does it because he has committed a crime, and he is reforming."

Alvin looked quickly at Oodlateeta. He didn't look dangerous. "What did he do?"

"When he was a teenager, he stole money."

"I thought the Inuit didn't need money."

Fox laughed. "Who told you that? Everyone needs

money for petrol. And other things cost money, too. Oodlateeta used money for drugs and liquor."

"What's that got to do with Pond Inlet?"

"We give a choice to young people who commit a crime. They can go to prison. Or they can go to Iqaluit and take classes about our people's traditional ways. About the weather, the tides, plants that can be used as medicines. About our people's history. Then they are brought to outpost camps, far away from towns, where they learn traditional skills."

"Why?"

"People who have skills and pride in their traditions do not need drugs. The young people who choose this program do not commit crimes again. Oodlateeta did the program years ago. Now he works for it. He teaches skills. We honor traditional ways here in Pangnirtung."

"Is he going to Pond Inlet to pick up a criminal?"

"People are not criminals. Their actions may be criminal, but they are simply people," said Fox. "The man is already here. Oodlateeta was planning to start training him in a couple of weeks. But he can start in a couple of days instead. Before Donald has a chance to figure out the plan.

"You shouldn't have to sneak around him. If he

shouldn't be in charge of me, he shouldn't be in charge of you.

"There is one church in town, with one missionary. Almost all of us are Christian. No one wants to fight Donald. But no one thinks he has the right to stop you, either. We will not say anything about your trip to him. By the time he finds out, there will be no point in arguing."

"So Oodlateeta and this other man and I will go by snowmobile to Pond Inlet?"

Fox laughed. "You will go by dog sledge."

Alvin could almost hear the low growl of the dogs outside. He tried to steady his heart. "Manitok said everyone uses snowmobiles now."

"That is true. And that is why everyone needs money for petrol. Most dog teams around here are used only for races these days—for fun and for shows for the tourists. But Oodlateeta works his team. That was the traditional skill that he learned from the Iqaluit program. He transports the young people to the outpost camps. And now and then he trains one of them to drive a team. The man with you on the sledge will be learning to drive the team."

"How far is it?"

"Nine hundred kilometers."

"How long will it take?"

"As long as it takes."

Alvin hugged himself. "How will I get north from there?"

"That is up to you." Fox stood. "And now we are going to have a special feast: walrus stew."

Walrus stew. Alvin shut his mouth tight.

"As the honored guest, you can have the eyes," said Fox. "It is tradition."

Alvin's stomach turned.

CHAPTER NINETEEN

Pond Inlet

Oodlateeta spoke no English. Neither did Akkavak, whose face showed no emotion. So whatever crime Akkavak committed was a mystery. He might have stolen a parka and breeches and *kamiks*—like Alvin sort of did, with Manitok. Or he might have done something violent. Maybe he murdered someone. But probably he'd have gone to jail for that. Probably murderers didn't get the choice of learning traditional trades. Alvin wished he had thought to ask Fox about Akkavak's crime before they'd started the journey. Now he was on the dog sledge and there was no one to ask. No one understood him.

But it would have been impossible to talk.
Oodlateeta needed to keep his voice strong for
shouting to the dogs. Oodlateeta would shout *"Ha-i,"*
and the dogs would go left. He'd shout *"U-va-i,"* and
the dogs would go right.

There were thirteen dogs fanning out from the
sledge. Oodlateeta had to keep the traces tight, or
they'd get tangled. It seemed every time they went
over an unexpected slope, the traces tangled anyway.
Then Oodlateeta would straighten them with bare
hands. It was a painstaking, slow job, and Oodlateeta
breathed hard on his hands to thaw them when he
finished.

Akkavak watched everything. By the second day,
Oodlateeta gave him short turns at the traces.

Oodlateeta sat on the front of the sledge, dressed
in a light-colored parka of animal skin with fringe
around the bottom and a huge puffy hood. His
breeches looked like they were made of polar bear
skin. They were fancier than Alvin's. Akkavak sat
behind Oodlateeta, dressed almost identically. That
was no surprise; Alvin had seen Aima give the outfit
to Akkavak before they left Pangnirtung.

The provisions were tied together behind
Akkavak. Much of it was food for the people and the

dogs, but some was staples for the people in Pond Inlet. And there were hastily thrown together presents for relatives. And a small box Fox added for someone named Idlouk Tana. Townsfolk wanted to take advantage of this trip—so many people that the start of the trip had to be delayed several days to give them all time to prepare things. Even the government took advantage: There was a letter for some lucky soul in Pond Inlet and a pack of letters that someone else would have to carry on by foot from Pond Inlet to Nanisivik, on the other side of the northern tip of Baffin Island. Normally that mail would have gone by a small postal service plane, but the next scheduled flight wasn't for more than a month.

At first Alvin had tried holding on to Akkavak, his arms encircling him from behind. That way he could see everything. But the cold wind rushing at his face was too much, even with his scarf tied around to cover his nose and mouth. And with his arms stretched out like that, he got cold all over fast. After that, he traveled balled up on the sledge, covered with a blanket, like another package.

The sledge would race along smoothly, and suddenly hit a bump and bounce hard. Sometimes it slithered to a halt on a crest of snow, then toppled over, going downhill in a short burst of tremendous speed. Alvin could hardly hold on. Often Oodlateeta got off to guide the sledge over rough terrain. Usually he made Akkavak get off with him, and sometimes he even made Alvin get off. At other times they'd run beside the sledge for no clear reason. But maybe it was just to get warm, because Alvin always felt revived after they'd done that.

They stopped frequently and Oodlateeta melted snow in tin cans over a Primus stove to make tea. That tea tasted wonderful. Alvin wished Grandma could have a cup.

Whenever they stopped, the dogs ate snow. Often they fought. The growls were bestial and their teeth ripped at one another. If it got too bad, Oodlateeta cracked the whip over the dogs' heads and they separated, though low growling sometimes continued for what seemed like hours. But the dogs never barked during the trip. It was as though the rule was to travel as quietly as possible.

In fact, traveling wasn't anywhere near quiet. The wind blew almost constantly, screaming across the ice, going directly from north to south. There was nothing to break its path. In those rare times when the wind would cease for a few hours, life felt suspended.

Alvin understood the lines on Oodlateeta's face now; the biting wind had etched its cry on his skin.

Most of the time the heaven above was pitch black, with nothing but stars to every side. But for a few hours each day the gray that hovered over the snow seeped everywhere and the world became dusky. There was a sunrise, even though no sunlight, with lovely warm yellows and oranges off to the east horizon. Along the west horizon were mountains, and on some days, when there were gaps in the mountains, Alvin could see just as lovely a sunset.

They stopped and camped according to some internal clock of Oodlateeta's body—a clock that Alvin's body couldn't make sense of. Alvin sometimes slept when they were traveling, and sometimes stared into the night when the others slept.

At those times he asked himself what he was doing here. Was he lost? He didn't feel like Alvin anymore. He didn't feel like anyone. He was, in fact, a lot like the packages on the sledge—simply there. It was as though he'd checked out of one life but hadn't managed to check into another yet. And the only thing that mattered in this in-between state was motion— they had to keep moving toward Pond Inlet. Motion meant life.

Oodlateeta had a knife he used for almost everything. He sharpened it on a file the first day, but then
the file got lost. They searched everywhere on the
sledge for it. After that, Oodlateeta sharpened the
knife on the hard sleeve of his parka. Alvin couldn't
believe that would work—but it did. A frozen hide
sleeve was as rough as a whetstone.

When they would stop to sleep, Oodlateeta and
Akkavak cut blocks of snow about four feet long and
two feet wide and arranged them in a circle. They
worked quickly and made a small dome with a short
tunnel opening. Alvin was eager to help, and soon he
was making the tiny igloos, too. Inside it was warm
enough from their body heat alone to take off their
outer clothing and sleep only in sweatsuits wrapped
in caribou-skin blankets. Oodlateeta always left an
opening in the roof. He stuffed a fur into it. After
they used the Primus stove for dinner, when the igloo
would begin to overheat, he'd pull out the fur till it
cooled off. Then he stuffed the hole closed again.

The dogs slept loose. A few times Alvin had to get
up to relieve himself while the others slept. The first
time he was so frightened of the dogs that he lay
awake trying to control himself, trying to fall back
asleep. But finally he had to go outside. He stepped

silently just beyond the tunnel opening and off to the side. The dogs didn't move. But when he turned around to look at them before he went into the igloo, twenty-six eyes shone at him through the black. And that happened every time; those dogs watched every move.

When the men woke for a new day, they lured each dog by holding out meat. As the dog jumped for the meat, Oodlateeta and Akkavak threw themselves on the dog and caught him by the throat. They slipped the harness over the dog's head and pushed the forepaws through. In the process Oodlateeta and Akkavak got minor wounds, which they licked, almost as though they were dogs, too.

Alvin huddled in the tunnel of the igloo during this. He wouldn't be of help if he stepped out there, but he felt guilty because he knew that even if he could have helped, he'd have been too afraid. It was enough that he had to be near the dogs—he couldn't touch them.

When all the dogs were harnessed, the lead dog gave a threatening growl and the others quieted down and obeyed Oodlateeta. Oodlateeta snapped that long, rawhide sealskin whip right over the lead dog's ear. All twenty-eight feet of it—Alvin had measured, using his own foot in the *kamik* as a measure for one foot. He admired the strength in Oodlateeta's wrists and elbows, and he was fascinated by Oodlateeta's right thumb. It was twisted and deformed from the strange way he wrapped the whip around it.

Akkavak didn't command the same respect from the dogs. They moved more slowly when he held the traces. But each day his turns at driving them grew longer, and gradually the dogs grew more responsive.

Oodlateeta and Akkavak and Alvin ate dried meats and fishes he couldn't recognize. Once they saw a seal lift its head right out of the snow. It took Alvin several minutes to realize it was a breathing hole in the ice—they were traveling over frozen sea. Oodlateeta stopped the dogs and took out his rifle. Then he changed his mind and they continued on. Later Alvin was sure he saw another seal ahead. He pointed and shouted, and a flock of ravens lifted into the air.

Akkavak carried a rifle, too. It seemed strange at first that he would have a rifle. But when Alvin thought about the rehabilitation program, it made sense. Oodlateeta treated Akkavak like a trustworthy person, and Akkavak acted like one.

The first night of the trip, Akkavak shot a goose. Oodlateeta drew out a tail feather and stuck it in the snow before they plucked the bird and cooked it.

The feather rose from the snow almost like a plant.

The stars never seemed to change, no matter how long they traveled and how often Alvin looked at them. But he knew they were going constantly north because of the flat horizon to the right—over the sea—and the mountains to the left. And, of course, that relentless northern wind.

And Alvin even knew how far they had gone each day, because when they stopped to sleep, he took the map Fox had given him out of his backpack and spread it in front of Oodlateeta. Then Oodlateeta placed his finger on the spot where they were.

Alvin studied the map. Pond Inlet was, by Alvin's reckoning, about two thirds of the way between Churchill and Eureka. After Oodlateeta dropped Alvin off at Pond Inlet—after they had completed the nine hundred kilometers from Pangnirtung to Pond Inlet—he would have only about another thousand kilometers to go.

A thousand kilometers. What was he thinking? The distances were enormous. And practically empty: In the entire eastern Canadian Arctic north of Pond Inlet, there were only two settlements. He stared at the map and wondered if he was losing his mind.

He usually fell asleep with his map under his cheek.

One time when they were sleeping, the dogs barked like maniacs. Oodlateeta and Akkavak grabbed their rifles. They went outside. Alvin crawled to the end of the tunnel. Akkavak's rifle went off. He must have shot right into the snow, because the air filled with a spray of shiny crystals. A huge polar bear lumbered off with the dogs barking behind him, staying at a respectful distance. The men came back inside and fell asleep instantly. Alvin stayed awake, listening for the dogs.

They passed several settlements, stopping to exchange news and share a meal. And they spent the night in two of them, sleeping on the floor of people's homes.

The first settlement they slept at was a lot like Pangnirtung—many houses and a church in the center. But the second settlement was tiny, just a scattering of homes. The villagers crowded into the home that hosted these visitors, and they stared at Alvin openly. They touched his cheek, one after the other, and murmured.

And they ate raw meat and raw fish.

Alvin watched in dismay. He'd managed to get out of eating the walrus eyes at the party Oodlateeta and his wife had thrown for him back in Pangnirtung by giving them, instead, to old Teenaq. Teenaq had cut open the eyes, licked away a clear liquid that he squeezed from them, chewed the black fleshy outer part, then finally eaten the small colorless ball in the center; and the whole time Alvin had watched in fascination, grateful for his escape. But he'd been forced to taste the walrus meat. And it turned out to be wonderful—sweet and rich and tender.

But now raw meat? Raw fish?

Alvin thought of all the bad things that live in flesh— the worms and bacteria. Mamma cooked meat well done. Still, he knew that some fancy restaurants served raw meat. And even raw fish. And these villagers looked healthy. Besides, traveling all day brought a ravenous hunger. And Matthew Henson would have satisfied his hunger in whatever way the people around him did. So Alvin chewed on dark fish meat and tried to fill his head with gratitude. It wasn't hard, really—the fish kept him alive. If he ate it fast, while it was still frozen, the taste was more delicate. But sometimes it was thawed; then he had to think about other things so he could almost ignore the strong, salty taste. Always he washed it all down with lots of that delicious tea.

Alvin played the pennywhistle at that first settlement on the sledge journey. When he finished, one of the men took a drum out of an animal-skin bag. Everyone sat on furs on the floor, silent, watching. The man drummed and sang to himself as he danced in the little opening at the center of the room. He played the same rhythm over and over and chanted. Now and then one hand would fly up, making circles in the air. And whenever the man cried out *"Ajaja,"* the women repeated it.

After a while Alvin got the courage to try following the drumbeats with the pennywhistle. No one made any special sign when he started, neither of disapproval nor of appreciation. But there was no tension in the air. He was sure they accepted his contribution. It amazed him that he could blend into something so foreign from his home. Here he was, way up in the Arctic, and he wasn't lost, after all. He felt part of their world.

But the next morning they were traveling again, part of nothing but the cold, which got noticeably fiercer with each day.

They passed no trees. If there were trees, any of those dwarf Arctic willows Alvin had read about back in the Sixteenth Street library, they were totally covered by the ice and snow. Or maybe they were already so far north, they'd passed the tree line.

Not once did it snow. Alvin was surprised. He'd

expected that the farther north you went, the more you'd be in snow day by day. Instead the air was dry. And unrelentingly cold. On those rare occasions when Alvin stuck his face out from his hood, he was blasted by the ferocity of the cold. Once Oodlateeta gave Alvin something hot to drink that tasted bitter and smelled disgusting. Alvin spat automatically. The wad of spit rolled when it landed, frozen before hitting the ground.

Finally one day, after they'd been traveling several hours, Oodlateeta shouted and pointed up ahead to the left. *"Takugii!"*

Akkavak shouted too. *"Takugii, takugii!"*

Alvin uncurled himself and looked. Huge black cliffs loomed through the gray air. "Pond Inlet?" asked Alvin.

"Ii," said Oodlateeta. "Yes!" He had been driving for the past several hours. But now he changed places with Akkavak.

Akkavak snapped his whip. *"Hut, hut, hut!"* he shouted to the dogs. He sat taller than ever, radiating pride at being able to drive into town in charge like that.

The cliffs were farther than Alvin had realized. It took hours to get there. Alvin couldn't tell how many, really. He had lost confidence in his sense of time. The lack of sunlight left him disoriented. The moon seemed to appear with no discernible pattern. The world felt endless. But they finally got there.

The houses in town had sealskins drying on the roofs. Alvin hadn't been able to see the roofs in Pangnirtung, because snow covered them. But here someone had cleared the snow from the roof of the largest building; the skins gave off a dark sheen in the moonlight. At the edge of the settlement was the usual open garbage heap.

Oodlateeta pointed to a home. Akkavak stopped the sledge in front of it. Oodlateeta pushed Alvin through an entrance tunnel like the ones they had built when they made igloos. But this wasn't an igloo—just a regular home. Alvin crawled into a tiny hall and stood up. On three sides hung animal skins from ceiling to floor. Oodlateeta and Akkavak crawled in behind Alvin and stood up. Oodlateeta lifted the skin in front of them. They entered a small room that had two wooden beds covered with layers of animal skins. An old man lay in one bed. An old woman sat on a chair.

The woman got up quickly and embraced Oodlateeta. Then she pushed the old man. He grumbled and rolled over. She pushed him harder till he fell out the other side of the bed. He stood up and hugged Oodlateeta. They talked and looked from Oodlateeta to Akkavak and Alvin, then back again. When they spoke to Akkavak, he said something back. No one spoke to Alvin.

Finally Oodlateeta motioned to Alvin to sit on the second bed. Oodlateeta and Akkavak left, and Alvin could hear them shouting to the dogs, settling them to sleep. The old woman sat back on her chair and the old man climbed into bed again. Alvin wished he knew how to speak in Inuktitut. They nodded at him and smiled. The man's teeth were discolored and several were missing. The woman had no front teeth at all. They kept nodding. Alvin nodded back. He felt ashamed to smile. He felt ashamed of having strong, white teeth—of having had all the advantages in life that had led to his strong, white teeth. He smiled a close-lipped smile and tried to use his eyes to show he was happy and grateful to be in their home. *"Qujannamik,"* he murmured every time someone looked at him.

Alvin was sweating inside his parka by the time Oodlateeta came back. He started to take off his hood, but Oodlateeta led him outside again. They went into another house.

A man welcomed Oodlateeta with a smile and a hug. He motioned for Alvin to take off his things. Alvin stripped down to his sweatsuit and *kamiks* and sat on a chair. A young woman and an older one sat on chairs. The young woman held a sleeping baby. She smiled at Alvin. There was a kerosene stove, like at Oodlateeta's home in Pangnirtung, and shelves stocked with cans of food. Voices came from a TV on top of a bureau. This family was better off than the families they had stayed with between Pangnirtung and here.

Oodlateeta stood by the door, with his parka still on. Alvin didn't understand why, and he couldn't ask. He looked at Oodlateeta. Then the door opened and another young man came in and embraced Oodlateeta. He took off his outer clothing and stood before Alvin. "I am Pauloosie," he said. "It is a pleasure to meet you, Kukukulik."

Alvin practically jumped at the sound of English after all this time. "Nice to meet you," he said with enthusiasm.

Oodlateeta hugged Alvin. Then he said to everyone, *"Tagvauvusi."* He turned and left.

Alvin looked at the door for a moment, then he realized it—this was the moment of parting. Alvin would be left in Pond Inlet with no idea of what to do next. His throat constricted in terror. "Isn't he coming back?"

"He must continue training Akkavak. They will sleep at his parents' home and leave in the morning," said Pauloosie.

"When will he come back?"

"In summer."

Of course. "It'll be a lot easier to ride the dog sledge in summer," said Alvin bleakly.

Pauloosie laughed. "It is impossible to travel that long distance by dog sledge in summer. It took you more than three weeks now. But in summer you'd have to go over land the whole way, not flat sea." He laughed again. "It would take double that."

They'd traveled for more than three weeks? Alvin knew it was a long time, but he hadn't thought it was that long. Why, by his calculations it was already the third week of February, then. The kids in his class were presenting their projects on African-American heroes.

And the dog sledge had gone over frozen sea the whole time, not just at the point when they'd seen the seal. Alvin hadn't known that, either. What else hadn't Alvin understood? He remembered that missionary saying how lucky he'd been to get this far alive. How many times had luck kept him alive on the sledge trip?

"No, Oodlateeta will fly here with Inukjuak," said Pauloosie, "the trapper who brought you to Pangnirtung."

Fox. Fox would be back, but not till summer. Alvin felt a small tremble in his cheeks. "Will anyone be going down to Pangnirtung before summer?"

"I think not," said Pauloosie. He looked at Alvin, but he didn't ask anything. The Inuit never seemed to ask anything. They just watched and somehow understood.

Alvin understood too—Pauloosie was waiting for him to say whether or not he'd changed his mind. Had he? Did he want to go back with Oodlateeta? No. Yes. He didn't know. "The postal plane will come soon, right?"

"It will come a few times before summer. But it does not carry passengers."

Alvin looked down. His hands lay limp in his lap.

The baby snuffled, and the mother shifted her position in the chair.

"They told me you were going north," said Pauloosie. "Oodlateeta spoke of your family."

Alvin looked at him wordlessly. When this whole thing began, he knew it would take time. But he hadn't thought in terms of months. He was going to go as far north as he could on the money he had—that was all. He never thought he'd get this far. Not really.

The Arctic was a dream.

A dream that came true.

And now he'd be locked in till summer.

The young woman got up and filled a cup from a pot. She handed Alvin the steaming broth. The rich smell of walrus saturated his nose; he took the broth gratefully. *"Qujannamik,"* he said.

She smiled.

"There is seaweed, too. Do you want some?" asked Pauloosie.

"Maybe later," said Alvin quickly. He drank the broth.

"Play for us, Kukukulik. Will you?"

Alvin took out his pennywhistle. He played slow and sweet.

When he finished, Pauloosie said, "It is my privilege to help you go where you want to go next." He waited expectantly.

Though Alvin heard the words, it took a moment before they made sense to him. Fox had said the next step would be up to Alvin—but now here was a man offering to help, just like that.

So he had to choose. Where was he going next?

Mamma's blackest eyes shined with tears inside his head. He'd come so far, and it had been so hard. She'd be astounded at what he'd done already. And she'd want him to come home now. To leave this frozen, bare world. Fast.

Everything here was unfamiliar and dangerous. A person could freeze to death just walking to the store. If there was a store here to walk to.

Where was the fierce beauty that Henson spoke of? Where was the lure that tugged at Matthew Henson's heart?

Alvin had no idea.

But he knew that something was ahead. He had to find out just how much he could do, how far he could go. The Arctic might not connect to his ordinary life in any way that made sense, yet somehow it had become essential. If Alvin could do this, he'd be different. Changed. Oh, how much he needed a change.

And that was why he couldn't turn back. That was exactly why. That was what he yearned for. It would be brutal to make Mamma and Grandma wait till summer, not knowing what had happened to him. So he'd write to them. Immediately. And that would have to be enough. Because he couldn't deny himself this chance. The need to press on was stronger than anything else he'd felt in his whole life.

"You ever heard of Matthew Henson?" asked Alvin at last.

"No," said Pauloosie in a quiet voice. All the Inuit Alvin had met spoke quietly.

"He went to the North Pole," said Alvin.

"Many white men have tried to do that," said Pauloosie. "Mostly they are crazy."

"He wasn't white. He was black like me. And he wasn't crazy." Alvin felt woozy with the desire to make Pauloosie understand. "He took an Inuk wife in Greenland. Well, they didn't have a wedding ceremony—and it wouldn't have been legal anyway, because he was married to an American woman named Lucy. But they had a child. Anaquak Henson was born in 1906. And Anaquak had five children. All boys. And they had children, too." Alvin paused to catch his breath, he'd been talking so fast.

Pauloosie stared at him with a stunned look.

Alvin almost laughed. He must have seemed totally nuts to Pauloosie. He forced himself to speak slowly. "They live here. Well, maybe not right here in Pond Inlet. But they live far north." Alvin put his hand to his forehead. His brain hurt from trying to say things right. "Matthew Henson understood things. I want to understand things like he did. I want to see what he saw." He clenched his jaw in frustration. What a stupid way to put it.

But Pauloosie didn't laugh at Alvin. He seemed to think this over. "Describe him to me, this Matthew Henson."

"He had a bushy mustache."

"The Inuit have almost no hair on their face," said Pauloosie. "If we do have a mustache, it's thin." He pulled on his chin as though he was pulling on a beard.

"And he was very tall," said Alvin.

"Tall?" Pauloosie looked up. "Tall with bushy hair on his face?" He talked to the man and women in rapid Inuktitut. Then he turned to Alvin. "We may know one of his descendants."

Alvin's skin turned goose bumps. "Really?"

"A man who is part Inuk and part not. Tall, with a beard. He is Idlouk Tana. He is the one who gathers feathers."

Alvin recognized the name. "That's the person Oodlateeta brought a box for. My friend Fox sent it."

"Yes. Idlouk Tana. Yes."

CHAPTER TWENTY

Stars

Alvin and Pauloosie stopped walking. They stood on the open expanse and faced each other. The black cliffs near Pond Inlet were behind Pauloosie. The huge tower of Mount Thule on Bylot Island was behind Alvin.

"Aksunai," said Pauloosie. "You go now."

Pauloosie had told Alvin much in the past several days, so he knew they'd part like this. Still, the reality was harsher than the thought. He didn't want to be alone outside, even for a short while. The power of the Arctic was clear: If you weren't alert, if you made a mistake, it could be disastrous. "Come with me."

"Idlouk Tana would never show himself if two people came together."

Alvin knew this, too. Idlouk Tana was a hermit. He left feathers in plastic bags for Pauloosie to pick up at this very spot. And Pauloosie brought him provisions and left them in this very spot on appointed dates. Rarely did anyone see Idlouk Tana face-to-face. But sometimes in the summer they saw him from a distance.

There was no choice: Alvin had to go on alone from here. He wore almost all of his clothes under his parka and breeches so that he had room in his backpack for the small box from Fox plus the provisions that Pauloosie was sending to Idlouk Tana. Idlouk Tana didn't expect these provisions yet, though. Alvin was going earlier than the appointed date. That's why he couldn't just sit at the regular exchange spot and wait. Idlouk Tana might not come. Instead Alvin had to go in search of his home.

"Will I ever see you again?" asked Alvin.

"*Immaqa,*" said Pauloosie. "Maybe." He looked past Alvin. Then he looked back. "*Kisiane immaqa nagga.* Maybe not."

"What'll I do if I don't find Idlouk Tana?"

"He will find you."

"What if he doesn't?"

"He will."

They'd been through all of this a dozen times, but Alvin never felt reassured. "Please, Pauloosie. I don't know the ways of this place. You can wander around without knowing where you are, but I can't."

"No Inuk wanders in winter without knowing where he is," said Pauloosie. "*Piusiunngituk.* It is not the custom."

"Then I can't do it, either," said Alvin desperately. "I need someone to make sure I'm safe."

Pauloosie spread his arms and turned in a circle. "See the stars?"

"They're everywhere. How could I miss them?"

"They are the spirits of our ancestors. They will look after you."

"Maybe your ancestors won't care about me," said Alvin.

Pauloosie laughed. "All human beings share the same ancestors. They will hold you till Idlouk Tana comes for you. He knows everything that happens near his home."

"Where is his home?"

"He comes from the direction of the mountain. Just keep going forward."

A sudden question came to Alvin: "Does he speak English?"

"I don't know. But you will make yourself understood."

How? Alvin sighed. "Don't forget to mail my letter." That letter to Mamma and Grandma was short—mainly just a statement of how much he loved them both. Still, it was important. After all, anything could happen.

Pauloosie patted his right pocket, where he'd put the letter. "It will go on the next postal-service plane."

"*Qujannamik.* Thank you for everything."

"You are very welcome, Kukukulik," said Pauloosie. He handed Alvin his walking pole. "Take this. Poke it into the snow as you go. If it doesn't feel like firm ground underneath, go a different way. *Aksunai.* Farewell for now." Pauloosie turned and swiftly headed back toward the black cliffs and his home.

"*Qujannamik,*" called Alvin after him, even though he was sure Pauloosie couldn't hear him. He clutched the walking pole tight.

Mount Thule stood tall on Bylot Island, across the narrow sound from Pond Inlet. Alvin turned and walked toward the mountain, poking in several places before each step. Pauloosie had assured him that the sound was frozen so deep, it was completely safe to walk across. So the walking pole must be for use on Bylot Island. Why? If there wasn't firm ground under the snow on the island, what was there? But it was too late to ask.

Long ago the Inuit had lived on Bylot Island. They had hunted the caribou with bows and arrows for generations. Then the white men gave them rifles. Within a few years, the Inuit had wiped out the entire caribou population. The Inuit of Bylot Island had to cross the sound in winter, when it was frozen solid, leaving behind the home their ancestors had known for hundreds of years, and make a new home on the much larger Baffin Island.

These days no Inuit lived on Bylot Island. Now and then in winter, trappers crossed the sound in search of the white fox and ermine that quickly overran the island once the people had left. And sometimes in summer, people hunted the caribou that had just as quickly come back to the island. But not often. The only person who lived on Bylot year-round was Idlouk Tana.

Pauloosie had told Alvin all this.

Alvin walked on hard snow, pressing the pole down decisively. He looked ahead at Mount Thule, which rose more than a mile straight up. It resembled a huge pyramid, inky black against the starry sky. He wanted to see how beautiful it was—he wanted to appreciate it like

Matthew Henson would have. But it just seemed stark. Almost ugly.

He walked as long as he could. Finally he stopped and rested. He wished he had some of the hot tea that Oodlateeta made on their long dog-sledge trip from Pangnirtung to Pond Inlet. It was very cold, but not as cold as it had been. Pauloosie had kept Alvin at Pond Inlet until a frigid front had passed. Today was supposedly a warm day, according to Pauloosie. Whether that meant twenty degrees below or seventy below, Alvin didn't know. He couldn't tell the difference. He only knew that without all his protective clothing, he'd die before an hour was up. Maybe long before. Pauloosie had given him a fox-skin vest that he wore under his parka. It was brown, because the fox had been trapped in warm weather, when it had its summer coat.

Alvin rested standing up, his arms against his sides. Pauloosie had told him that if you separate your arms from your sides, they lose heat fast. But Alvin had already learned that for himself on the dog-sledge trip. Pauloosie had also warned him not to sit in the snow. So Alvin jogged from foot to foot to keep warm.

A gust of wind filled the air with glittering snow dust. He stopped and stared. Back home Shastri's father ran a furniture factory, and even when the saws weren't running, the air was filled with yellow specks of sawdust. Right now Alvin felt like Bylot Island was a giant diamond factory.

Something moved. He held his breath. It was a white snow hare. One shiny black eye looked at him. Then it hopped off.

That must have meant Alvin was either on land or close to it. He turned his face upward. The wind had died just as fast as it came up, but a slight breeze remained, and he easily determined that it was coming from behind him. Pauloosie had told him that when the wind is behind you, the nearest land is ahead, not behind you, even if you are walking on frozen water. So he was almost there. Alvin shuffled again. He shuffled and shuffled and shuffled, leaning on his pole.

Eventually he had to rest. He didn't want to. The mountain was close now; the land had started to rise. Idlouk Tana's home couldn't be too much farther. But he was exhausted. Doing anything outdoors in this cold was such hard work that a person couldn't keep it up for long.

Alvin dropped his backpack with a loud crunch of hollow snow. It was too heavy. He would leave it here and find it again later. He reached inside and took out his pennywhistle. The parka had no pockets, so he slid the pennywhistle inside through the opening at the neck. He was packed so tight into the parka that the pennywhistle wedged there, against his chest.

He felt strange. As though something was watching him. He turned very slowly. A white-gray dog stared at him. The amber, wide-set eyes glowed through the dark. Its tail was bushy. Its ears came to sharp points. Its muzzle was long. Its coat was shabby. And then the stark realization struck him: This was an Arctic wolf. But before he could run, the wolf disappeared. Just like that—gone.

Alvin shuffled as fast as he could. Anything could come at him. Wolves. Polar bears. Anything. He couldn't hear well with the hood over his ears. Maybe there were steps behind him, coming at him. Oh, no. No no. He shuffled faster. He ran. He ran and ran and fell. He rolled onto his back and held his walking pole across his chest with both hands like a cudgel, prepared to fight.

The moon appeared white and brilliant straight above Alvin's head. A vague rainbow formed, spreading out slowly, making a halo of all the colors. It flared upward into an arch that absorbed the halo and came sprinkling down like a huge curtain. The air everywhere was yellow and green. It shimmered as far as he could see. At the edges it was blue. And now red. And so much yellow. Silent waterfalls of color cascaded until the entire heaven danced with glossy sheets of flame down to the horizon on all sides.

He thought about Grandma in church, belting out those hymns of praise for glory. This was what *glory* meant. This was sublime.

Despite the terrifying cold, Alvin took out his pennywhistle, ripped off his mittens and scarf, and blew a long, loud, clear note into the dazzling sky. It lingered there as though it was alive, as though it belonged in this holy place.

And with that pure sound, Alvin realized that if he didn't get up fast, he might never be able to play such a note again. And if he didn't get up fast, he would have achieved nothing—nothing at all. Except to show that Mamma's fears were right. But they weren't right. This sky proved that. This glorious sky. And if he didn't get up fast, he'd never get back to Mamma and Grandma, so that he could tell them that, so that he could describe this fierce beauty.

Alvin put his pennywhistle back inside his shirt. He tied his scarf around his mouth, put up his hood, and pulled on his mittens. Yes. He hauled himself to his feet and brushed the snow off his breeches. Yes and yes. He stamped in a small circle to get his circulation going again. Oh, yes.

He looked around. The wolf was nowhere to be seen.

But somewhere out there was Idlouk Tana.

He walked on through the snow, poking with his walking pole. On and on, chanting "yes" inside his head.

A hiss intruded on his chant.

But the wind hadn't picked up.

He slogged on.

The hiss grew closer, louder. It became a shriek. And it was coming from the rising slope ahead.

It could be anything—anything. But Alvin had to take a chance. He pulled down his scarf and shouted. "Hello! Hello, hello, hello, hello!"

As though emerging from the mountain itself, a huge hairy monster came sliding down toward Alvin. No, not sliding, gliding fast, a half foot above the snow. Flying!

Alvin would have run if he could. But it took all his energy just to remain standing and not faint dead away.

CHAPTER TWENTY-ONE

Idlouk Tana

The stone walls were dark, smoke stained. Turf wedged tight between the stones. The corners of this small room showed white. The air was warm and humid.

Alvin sat on a raised platform. The monster, who turned out to be a man with a blanket wrapped around his shoulders on a sled made of clear ice, had led him inside through the customary tunnel, and then gone off for a while, returning with Alvin's backpack. He was a broad man with a long gray beard, and right now he was squatting by a glass fish tank full of fluff the color of his beard. He studied a thermometer attached to the bottom of the tank. He hadn't spoken at all to Alvin since they'd first met. Instead he'd gone about his business as though Alvin didn't exist.

Alvin hadn't spoken, either. He was so cold and so stunned at the appearance of the man that it was enough just to come inside and warm up and watch. But this couldn't go on forever. "Idlouk Tana?" said Alvin hesitantly. "Is that who you are?"

The man kept his eyes on the tank. "Did you come looking for me?" He spoke English, very clear English, though with a slight stiffness.

The rush of relief made Alvin feel weak all over again. "Yes."

"I took you in because otherwise you'd die. But you must return to wherever you came from."

"You ever heard of Matthew Henson?" Alvin listened to his own question—the question he'd asked repeatedly. How absurd it seemed.

"Of course." The man stirred the feathers.

Of course? Alvin could scarcely believe his ears. He leaned forward eagerly. "Are you related to him? Really?"

"No."

"Then how do you know about him?"

"You know about him. Are you related to him?" Idlouk Tana's voice was flat.

"I'm sorry. I didn't mean to make you mad. No one I've met in the north so far ever heard of him, is all."

"Canadians don't celebrate him. They don't celebrate any Americans."

"Oh." Celebrate. What a funny way to say it. "When I described Matthew Henson, Pauloosie thought you might be one of his descendants."

Idlouk Tana adjusted a dial on the tank. "Matthew Henson's descendants live in Greenland. They've always lived in Greenland. And if you're looking for them, you might as well not ask, because I can't help you get to Greenland. All I can do is send you back where you came from."

Idlouk Tana stood up. He was well over six feet tall, and he had a paunch. He sat on the edge of the platform and looked straight ahead, at nothing. His eyes were a washed-out color, almost like a milky sky. He seemed remarkably old. And his face showed no interest in Alvin.

Alvin looked around the walls again. Strips of dried fish hung in one corner. He sniffed. They had been smoked. In another corner were metal traps, ropes, a bow and arrows. He almost smiled. He'd always wanted to learn to use a real bow and arrow. Everything about this home felt timeless, as though people had lived in it the same way forever. "What's the white in the corners?" he asked.

Idlouk Tana didn't blink. "I live here alone because that's what I want. You're going tomorrow."

Alvin hadn't said he wanted to live with Idlouk Tana. But the words reverberated inside him insistently. He had experienced two mortal dangers already—on the train to Churchill and out in the open here on Bylot Island. He wasn't about to risk a third—after all, three strikes and you're out. This was as far north as Alvin was going. And he needed a home until summer—a home where he could learn things, like how to use that bow and those arrows.

He hugged himself and looked around the room again. "I'd make myself useful," said Alvin. "I'd do whatever you need done."

"Chores keep me alive. I need no one."

Alvin wanted to plead. But the firm set of Idlouk Tana's shoulders forbade him. Alvin's snow gear and backpack lay on the floor beside the platform. But they wouldn't stay there. Somehow Idlouk Tana would return Alvin and all his stuff to Pauloosie. It seemed wrong, like one giant failure. This was where Alvin and all his stuff should stay—right here.

He reached inside his shirt and took out his pennywhistle. He played "Georgia on My Mind." He needed his favorite song and only his favorite song. He played over and over, letting the pennywhistle sing all the sadness inside him.

Idlouk Tana had dropped his head, chin almost to chest, at the first notes. But soon he raised his head, and his nearly colorless eyes glistened. He stood and reached into a large animal-skin pouch that hung from the ceiling over the platform. He took out a violin and accompanied Alvin.

Together the pennywhistle and the violin wept the loneliness of an icy world.

But another element crept gradually into the music. The instruments sang now of seals that pop up out of the frozen sea for a breath, and birds that nestle in flocks, and the hare, and the wolf, and all the different peoples in this world.

After a long while, Alvin stopped playing.

Idlouk Tana rested his violin on his lap. "The white in the corners . . . " He pointed to the white Alvin had asked about. "That white is bone. I made this house of stone and whalebone, held together with sod. People in Greenland used to live in stone houses like this. An old man taught me the ancient ways of building when I was a boy."

"How old?"

"About your age."

"Have you lived here ever since?" asked Alvin.

Idlouk Tana shook his shaggy head.

"Are you from Greenland, then?"

"I was born in Iceland."

Alvin swallowed. "You don't look like the Arctic people I've seen so far."

"My father was from Denmark. My mother was a Greenlandic Inuk. We moved to Greenland when I started school."

"And that's where you learned how to build this house," said Alvin softly, looking around in admiration.

"My grandfather taught me."

"I could have guessed. I have a grandmother. A great-grandmother, really."

Idlouk Tana stood up and put the violin back into its pouch. Then he sat on the edge of the platform again.

"You're tall for someone half Inuk. And you're pale," said Alvin.

"All of me is turning gray now, fading." Idlouk Tana ran the fingers of his right hand over the skin of his left forearm. His fingers were gnarled and twisted. But it wasn't from a dog-sledge whip—it was different from the way Oodlateeta's fingers were twisted.

"What happened to your fingers?"

"I collect driftwood in summer to use for heat in fall and winter. But there's never enough to last. So most of the year I make fires from dried moss and lichen. Ripping lichen off the stone year after year does nasty things." Idlouk Tana held his hands in front of his face, palms cupped upward, as though he was amazed at the sight of himself.

"You still play the violin good."

"Music is the only way to stay sane through winter," said Idlouk Tana.

Alvin nodded in a rush of understanding. That's why his pennywhistle had paved the way for him with the Inuit. What blind luck that that little boy on the train had left it behind.

"A great singer made that song you played famous. Ray Charles."

"But Louis Armstrong sang it even better," said Alvin.

Idlouk Tana smiled. "You say his name right. That's what he called himself: Louis, with an *s* at the end."

"I know," said Alvin.

"He died before you were born. Who told you how he said his name?"

"I heard a recording of him singing 'Hello, Dolly!' In it he says, 'This is Louis,' with an *s*. So I know."

Idlouk Tana gave an appreciative *humph*. "Are you hungry?"

"Always."

Idlouk Tana laughed. He put on a parka and breeches.

"Where are you going?" asked Alvin.

"If I'm lucky, we'll have seal for dinner."

CHAPTER TWENTY-TWO

Water and Cookies

Idlouk Tana carried in the great block of ice. Alvin carried the sack of lichen they had just gathered. Together they put the ice block in a giant pot over a fire. Idlouk left tending the fire to Alvin, which was no problem. He knew well how to feed it with the lichen and lie on his belly and blow low and steady. Idlouk had shown him. He'd been here awhile—he wasn't sure how many days, but it was at least a week already. He knew how to do lots of chores.

This ice was bluish. It was seawater that had melted a little during the summer, until the salt was just about gone. Idlouk said it would taste like fresh-water. Alvin watched it lose the blue tint as it melted.

They drank from stone bowls.

"It's delicious," said Alvin. Then he laughed. That sounded crazy. How could water be delicious? But what they had been drinking before was old and stale compared to this new water.

Idlouk smiled and raised his bowl in a toast. "To sweet water."

That's how they generally talked. A few words from Alvin. A few words from Idlouk. Nothing extra. That was Idlouk's way.

Alvin raised his bowl toward Idlouk's with a smile. They savored every drop in companionable silence. Then they stacked their bowls on a shelf.

Alvin swept the unused lichen back into the sack and emptied the sack into a box against the wall. The box was already half full. Idlouk liked to collect lichen for every fire he built, so long as the weather was good. And he always gathered extra, even though it was such hard work, because he wanted to add to the cache. That way if he needed a fire in the middle of a storm, he could just reach into the storage box.

Most of the lichen in the box was grayish green. And most of what Alvin dumped in now was the same. But some tumbled out orange. Bright orange. Almost everything they brought inside from the dark turned out to be a dull color or just white. But not this lichen. It was beautiful.

Mamma and Grandma would want to know about that. They'd want to know his amazement. He hated the idea that they might think he was lost or miserable or dead. He had to remember to tell them about the lichen in his next letter. He wrote to them a lot. Sometimes in the morning before Idlouk woke. Sometimes in the night, after dinner. But every day, no matter what.

He couldn't mail the letters, though. Not until it was time for Idlouk's next drop-off of feathers to Pauloosie. And that wouldn't be for a month. So he kept the letters in his notebook. In the meantime he tried to communicate with Mamma and Grandma through his thoughts so they wouldn't worry. Grandma always said that if two people were thinking about each other at the same time, then somewhere they were together. So if Mamma or Grandma was thinking about him any of the thousands of times he thought about them, maybe they could hear him somehow. Maybe in their dreams, because he dreamed about them a lot. If they could hear him now, he'd say, "Mamma, listen to Grandma. Believe her. She knows it'll be okay." And he'd say, "I miss you. Everything here is new and that makes it exciting. But I still miss you. Every day." And he'd tell them about this lichen.

But, especially, he'd tell them about this water. He realized today was the first time he'd really loved something on this trip. It was only water, but he loved it. Other things had scared him or amazed him—like the sky and the endless stretches of snow and the wild ocean. But those things were so huge, you couldn't understand them. The water was different. It was right there, right inside him. It felt clean, like everything about it was pure, the way the world was supposed to be. Today he could taste in the water why he came here.

He wanted Mamma and Grandma to know that.

Idlouk Tana stood up and stretched. "Shall we celebrate the water?"

"Sure. How?"

"Cookies."

Alvin jumped to his feet. "I didn't think you had junk food." He scanned the shelves for telltale cellophane packaging. The last cookies he'd eaten were those Oreos on the train to New York. He had thought he'd never want cookies again in his whole life. But now the idea sounded great. "What kind?"

"Bear."

Alvin shut his mouth.

Idlouk opened sacks by the wall. "Flour. Sugar. Powdered eggs. Powdered milk." He put a deep wooden bowl on the floor in front of Alvin. "Start mixing. I'll be right back."

"How much do I put of each thing?"

"Use your common sense." Idlouk left.

Alvin was no stranger to cooking. And he'd made cookies with Mamma before. But they always used a recipe. He couldn't remember the first thing about those recipes right now, though. Well, all right, he had common sense; he could figure it out. What should he measure with? His stone bowl, sure. Flour had to be the biggest ingredient. So he put in two bowls of flour. And sugar, sugar had to be pretty important in cookies. He put in a bowlful. Eggs? He thought maybe a recipe at home called for an egg or two. So he put in part of a bowl. And part of a bowl of milk. He stirred the powdery mixture with a wooden spoon.

Idlouk came in with two roughly cut cubes of gray-ish white stuff. He placed one on the floor. Then he put the other one into a pan and stuck it on the embers of the fire. The cube melted into clear liquid that smelled sort of like beef.

"Bear fat?" asked Alvin.

"Polar bear fat. From the meat locker." The insulated box outside the tunnel opening was their meat locker. Idlouk looked over at the bowl of powder mix. "Just about the right amount, too."

Alvin hugged himself instinctively at the words polar bear. So far he'd seen only little animals on Bylot Island, nothing threatening. Except for the wolf on the first day he got here. "Are there lots of polar bears here?"

"None. At least none for now. They've gone south."

Alvin let out a little moan of relief. "I guess it's too cold even for polar bears."

"Polar bears can withstand any cold. Their fur and fat keep them so warm that sometimes they overheat just from swimming, so they roll in the snow to cool down. No, the bears went south to find food, because most of their prey went south. They'll be back in summer, when the caribou return."

"Oh." Summer on Bylot. Would Alvin really still be here?

Idlouk gestured toward the spoon with his chin. Alvin picked it up and stirred while Idlouk poured the melted polar bear fat into the bowl. "Shape them onto this, while I get the stove going." He put a pan by Alvin's feet and went to the little stone stove in one corner.

Alvin made the cookies the size of his palm and watched Idlouk put the other white cube of fat into the bottom of the stone stove and set it on fire. "Cookies made with bear fat, baked over a bear fire. Bear cookies, all right."

"The burning fat is caribou, not bear," said Idlouk. "It gives off a low flame—that's the best for baking." He slid the pan into the stove.

This was the first time they'd used that stove. "Is that stove only for baking?"

"Pretty much. It's been in my family for genera- tions." Idlouk settled with his back against the bed platform and his long legs stretched out in front.

The smell of the cookies permeated the air already. Floury and meaty at the same time. Alvin was glad there wouldn't be any polar bears till summer. That meant all he had to watch out for were the wolves. "I haven't seen a wolf since the day I came to Bylot."

Idlouk looked at him. Then he shut his eyes. For

a moment Alvin thought he might fall asleep. But then he said, "Wolves run away unless they're in a pack, and even then they won't bother you if you don't attack them. When I was a kid, I had a wolf as a pet. I trained it to carry a pack, but I could never train it to pull a sledge."

A wolf for a pet. It was hard to imagine. Alvin moved over beside him and stretched out his own legs.

"Then one day a man killed my wolf for the fur. He gave me money. I was sad, but I took the money and gave it to my mother." He stopped talking.

"That's awful," said Alvin.

"These days it's illegal to keep wild animals as pets, even way up here."

"I'm glad."

Idlouk opened his eyes. "Auoooo," he howled. "Try it, Kukukulik."

"Auoooo," howled Alvin.

"If you howl like a wolf, they'll be tricked and you can get close enough to almost touch them."

"I'd never be brave enough to touch a wolf, but it's cool to think I could."

"It's useful to know how to get close to the animals. If you lie on your stomach on the ice and scrape with both hands, seals will think you're like them, and then you can crawl right up to their breathing hole to spear them."

The very idea of his belly on ice made Alvin shiver. "What other animals can you get close to?"

"Watch them and learn for yourself. That's the best way."

Sort of like primary research, like what Ms. Artiga back home wanted his class to do. Only for Idlouk it wasn't research, it was life.

Idlouk went to the stove and took out the cookies.

Alvin held a hot cookie and hesitated, while Idlouk took a bite of his. "Are they okay?"

Idlouk took another bite. And another. He finished the cookie and reached for a second. "From now on this is your job. You make them better than me. Sweeter. And they crumble better in my mouth."

Alvin grinned. He took a bite of his cookie. It was dense and firm. And it was good. In fact, it was great.

"We'll need a batch every other day. We can carry them with us whenever we go outside, for quick energy." Idlouk leaned back against the bed platform again. "Your turn."

Alvin knew what Idlouk meant: What Idlouk had

told him about having a wolf for a pet was a kind of story. Now it was his turn to tell a story. He pushed a cookie crumb from the corner of his mouth onto his tongue. "Once I found a bird nest . . . "

CHAPTER TWENTY-THREE

Words in the Air

Dear Mamma and Grandma,

Tonight Idlouk and I told each other stories again. We do it every night. We didn't used to. The first two days I was here, Idlouk was quiet all the time. But on the third day he started talking. He said it was like he'd forgotten how to be with people and then he remembered. Outdoors we still go silent most of the time, but indoors sometimes he talks a lot and other times he's quiet.

In homes like this one, traditional homes, there are no walls separating people. Idlouk says one of the bad things about modern homes is that the inner walls separate people so they don't spend long nights telling stories anymore.

Idlouk's stories are mostly about animals. But sometimes they're about people who make mistakes. Usually the people get angry or impatient, so they don't think straight and they wind up getting lost in the snow or having an accident and freezing to death. These are the stories people up here tell children. They aren't the best stories. But I understand why people tell them. In this kind of cold, you have to think straight.

We take turns telling them. When it's my turn, I talk about you two. Or Uncle Pete. And sometimes I talk about the kids at school. Especially Shastri. Once I couldn't think of a story, but Idlouk told me to keep talking, so I told the baby story of "The Three Little Pigs." It was stupid, but Idlouk liked it. I like the whole thing—the whole storytelling thing. It's more talking than I ever do with my friends, so it felt weird at first. But then it felt good. I try to make my stories interesting. I try to surprise Idlouk.

When you read these letters, I bet they'll surprise you, too. And not just because of the things I say, but because I say so much. It's like I'm writing all my thoughts—like I want you to come inside me and make yourself at home.

Today there was a break in the dark. It was short, but it was real. Idlouk says the sun is coming back. I shouted for joy. I didn't realize how much I miss the sun until that measly bit of light. And it gave me a kind of calendar—it'll be spring soon. Not spring in terms of plants, but spring in terms of the calendar. Idlouk says I'll be sick of sun by summer. The summer sun shines all day long and all night long. I can't wait to be sick of sun. Washington, D.C., is a sunny place. I never realized that before.

Love,

Alvin

CHAPTER TWENTY-FOUR

Sledding

Alvin and Idlouk stood by a seal hole—an *aglu*—and peered down through the gray light into the black water.

"We still have meat left from the seal you killed a month ago, when I first got here," said Alvin. "So why do we need another?"

"We don't. I didn't bring the *unaaq*."

The *unaaq* was a harpoon made of a sharp bone blade. Idlouk had let Alvin hold it before. "So what are we doing here?"

"See." Idlouk pointed at the lines in the ice.

"Teeth marks from where the seal gnawed his way through."

The cloudy sea ice was thick. Maybe a whole foot thick. "He has strong teeth," said Alvin.

"It took him hours to gnaw through ice this thick. Other seals sometimes bash holes with their heads or simply find a crack in the ice and push it wider till they can come up through it. This seal is a worker. He's diligent."

If Alvin was a seal, he wouldn't bash his head like that. "Seals must not be too smart. I wonder how many knock themselves out and drown."

Idlouk swung a sledgehammer against the side of the hole. Over and over. Then he handed it to Alvin.

Alvin swung the hammer. Over and over. Sea ice was hard to break. It didn't shatter like fresh ice. Finally a chunk broke free from the side of the hole.

Idlouk scooped it up and turned it over. The underside was covered with gook. "Algae," he said.

They walked back to land with Alvin beside Idlouk. Usually Idlouk insisted that Alvin walk behind him, following in his footsteps. But when they walked on frozen sea, they could walk side by side.

They built a little fire outside the hut and made algae soup in a steel can and ate it right there. And it was good. Just about everything they ever ate was good.

Part of what made this so good was eating it outside. Alvin loved fires outside. The light seemed like moving paint on the gray wall of the air. The permafrost around the fire melted and froze again into a sheet as clear and slick as wet glass. He imagined he could see himself in it, like a mirror. But when he looked, only his shadow showed. It showed clearly; sunlight was coming.

Idlouk rapped his gloved knuckles on the ice. "Want to go sledding?"

The first time Alvin had seen Idlouk, he thought he was flying. But he was sliding on a sled. An ice sled. Alvin had watched in amazement as Idlouk got off the sled and simply abandoned it at the foot of Mount Thule. He wondered what it would be like to ride on one—but he hadn't had the nerve to ask, because it seemed like every time he asked about something, Idlouk would take him outside to learn for himself. And he wasn't sure he wanted to learn about ice sledding for himself. He looked at Idlouk cautiously.

But Idlouk was already tamping the permafrost with the sledgehammer as he walked backward in a straight line. Cracks in the ice shot out like bursts of stars. He measured out a rectangle about three feet wide by six feet long and kept tamping, around and around the perimeter, forming a groove of crushed ice. Then he went into the hut and came out with a shovel. He levered up one corner of the rectangle, and an ice block, about a hand's-width thick, rose up out of the ground. He pushed it sideways, and it slipped onto the ice next to the hole it had just come from.

They pushed the ice sled over the snow and went up the lower slopes of Mount Thule. "Get on," said Idlouk, holding the lower edge of the sled.

Alvin straddled the sled gingerly.

"Put your legs straight out in front."

So Alvin sat with his legs straight out. He looked past Idlouk at the long stretch to the bottom. The sun was bright now, so he could see that it was a clear path. But it was steep. The sled would go fast. He wanted to jump off.

Before he could do it, though, Idlouk stepped to one side. The sled slipped forward. Alvin didn't know where to grip. Idlouk jumped on behind as the sled went by. He put his legs outside Alvin's and held him around the waist, and they were off.

The sled picked up speed. The world became a

blur. It went so fast Alvin had to close his eyes or the wind would cut them. With his eyes closed it really did feel like flying. Or maybe like disappearing. Like becoming the wind they moved through.

The sled leveled out as it hit bottom, but it slid for a long way before it finally stopped. Without a word, they pushed it back up the slope. It was heavy. Then they went down again. They went down a dozen times.

"Hungry?" said Idlouk.

It seemed they'd just finished the algae soup, but Alvin realized his stomach was empty. And the sun was already fading. They must have been sledding for four or five hours.

Idlouk headed in the direction of the hut.

Alvin rubbed his aching arms. Then he pushed the ice sled.

"Leave it," said Idlouk.

"But can't we go sledding again tomorrow?"

"Depends on the weather. If it's too cold, you can lose your breath and die. Today was a little break in the cold—like the day you came to Bylot. Anyway, if we brought it home, it would only freeze to the ground overnight. It's just as easy to make a new one."

If they sledded in the coldest weather, they could lose their breath and die.

And that couple, Mark Seltzer and his wife, had died in fifteen-foot waves near here somewhere.

And in so many of Idlouk's stories, disobedient children wound up getting lost in the snow and disappearing.

Alvin walked closer to Idlouk.

Idlouk veered off the path. Alvin knew immediately that they were going to check a trap. He'd gone with Idlouk to set some the other day, simple snare traps.

Idlouk brushed the snow off the trap, revealing a ball of frozen brown fur with a short tail.

"A rat?" said Alvin.

"A lemming. There's a lot of them in tunnels under the snow."

"But how can they survive down there? What do they eat?"

"Frozen plants."

They went home and cooked the lemming over an open fire. It was good. Not like Grandma's special pork. And not like Mamma's Sunday chicken. Not juicy like that. The meat was lean and Alvin had to chew it a long time. But the taste was strong and satisfying.

And somehow it seemed right to have to chew it so long. Chewing felt like saying thank you to the animal for giving its life. It felt like praying.

After they cleaned up, Alvin took out his penny-whistle. Idlouk grabbed his violin—his fiddle, as he called it. Alvin taught Idlouk a marching song he'd learned for the play about the American Revolution. Idlouk taught Alvin a Danish song his father had taught him as a kid. Then they just made things up. Like jazz musicians. Now and then a long passage of their improvised jazz even sounded good.

When they put their instruments away, Alvin stretched and got ready for bed. He felt strong. He'd been with Idlouk less than a month, but it was long enough that their walks together in the snow had begun to change him. When he first came, a short walk put him out of breath fast. But today they had walked for hours, and he hadn't been tired in the least. Maybe by now he'd walked pretty much all over this island. "How large is Bylot Island?" he asked.

"About the size of the state of Connecticut." Idlouk had never been to the United States, but he had studied American geography in school, and he often said things about the states.

Alvin had studied American geography too, but he didn't really know how large Connecticut was. He'd seen it on maps; it was smaller than Virginia and smaller even than Maryland. But still, it had to be big. That meant Bylot Island was big. So he had seen only a tiny fraction of it.

That first day on Bylot, Alvin had walked the sound and hoped for Idlouk to find him. "Idlouk, how did you come across me the day I first came here? Was it by accident?"

"Not at all. I heard a blast from your pennywhistle. So I directed my sled toward the noise."

"What if you'd been way on the other side of the island? You wouldn't have heard me." By the time Idlouk would have found Alvin, he'd have frozen to death. He knew that for dead certain. He knew a lot about the cold and what it did.

"I'd never have been on the other side of the island in January. I don't stray far from home in the deep of winter."

The deep of winter. That seemed right. "Winter is deep here," said Alvin. "Like the snow."

"The next time it snows," said Idlouk, "we can go back to that seal hole. It'll be covered, and we can put feathers on top of the snow. When the seal comes up under the snow and puffs hard so he can breathe again, the feathers will move."

Dancing feathers. Alvin smiled. "That must be pretty."

"Inuit hunters do that, so they can get close without the seal seeing them and spear the seal right through the snow."

So it wasn't a game. It wasn't just for fun. Almost everything had a reason behind it. And the reason was almost always survival.

CHAPTER TWENTY-FIVE

Reverence

Dear Mamma and Grandma,

We left a package of feathers for Pauloosie today, but I decided not to mail these letters, after all. I'm sorry. I know you're worrying about me. I know that. When I sent the letter from Pond Inlet, I felt different. But now I know what I want. I want to stay here until summer. If I mailed more letters and if they actually reached you, Mamma would probably hand them to the police and soon some Canadian official would appear at Idlouk's home and take me back and then everything would be over before I was ready. Maybe that couldn't happen—because of how hard it is to get here and all—but I can't take the chance. I'll come back on my own when I'm ready. And I'm sorry for all the worry that's causing you. I'm sorry. But what else can I do?

Anyway, I'm still writing. And you can read all this when I get home.

The sun shone today for a long time. It's hard to guess, but I think it must have been six hours at the least. It's been shining a little bit more each day. I know that's happening at home too but here I notice it more, because before it was so dark and because the sunlight must increase by a quarter hour each day, so much more than at home. I love the light. So does Idlouk. We go outside several times a day, usually not for more than a half hour. But when the sun is out, we stay out the whole time, no matter how long it is. Last week we stayed out really long sledding.

If there's no wind, I love being outside in the cold. It allows me to think. To wonder. Sometimes I even wonder if the world I left behind still exists. I feel almost like a time traveler—like I've gone back zillions of years and maybe I'll never return.

Idlouk showed me photographs of his mother

when she was a girl. One of the women in the background had a baby on her back in a little pack. It's like a papoose built into her hooded parka. They call it an *amauti*. He said Inuit women carry small children on their backs so that if they fall into water, the baby gets out with them. Up here death is always waiting for you to make a mistake. Maybe that's how it is everywhere—like the changing of the sunlight. But you can't forget it here.

Right now I'm very glad I decided not to mail these letters. You'd be crying if you read what I just wrote.

But you'd be happy to know I've been praying. It's not normal prayers, not what you and Grandma do. It's little stuff. Sometimes I look at a thing—any old thing—a coil of rope, a fishing spear, a duck feather—anything—for a long long time. That's what I mean by praying. At least it feels like praying to me. Looking at things.

And chewing meat. Chewing and chewing, just to show gratitude.

There's another reason to chew, too. This is something you're not going to like to know, Mamma. But lots of the time we eat things raw. Especially fish. Idlouk says the nutrients in the raw flesh will keep a person healthy in the Arctic. In the old days the Inuit ate almost all their meat raw. And raw meat takes longer to chew. Or at least it takes me longer. I don't hate it. Sometimes it even tastes okay. But I have to chew slowly because there's no way to not think about the animal that died when you eat it raw. I have to pray extra.

And Idlouk and I play music—him on the fiddle and me on the pennywhistle. That's a kind of prayer.

An old man way back when I was traveling here gave me a special name because of that pennywhistle—it's Kukukulik. It means "the one who plays the flute." I told Idlouk. He says he respects the fact that you named me after the great modern dancer Alvin Ailey, but he prefers Kukukulik in the north. So that's what he calls me. But I'm still your Alvin.

We have a lot of games to pass the hours with. The one I love most goes like this: Idlouk puts something in his hand and spreads a cloth over it. Then I feel underneath and guess what it is. Sometimes I'm right, too. Then I do it to him. He's always right. He takes his time before he guesses. He likes to be sure. You'd be good at this game, Mamma.

Love,

Alvin

CHAPTER TWENTY-SIX

Full Attention

Alvin opened the huge canvas bag. Little puffs of duck down floated up and made him sneeze. He put several large handfuls into a giant stone bowl and got to work picking out the stones, dirt, sand, twigs, and bits of eggshell. This was his routine, although he usually did it side by side with Idlouk. But when he woke this morning, Idlouk had already gone out. So he decided to begin on his own.

Last spring and summer Idlouk had collected these feathers from the nests of eider ducks. After picking out all the debris, Idlouk and Alvin would put the feathers in a special heated aquarium that Idlouk had rigged up for sterilizing them. Then they'd pack the clean feathers in bags. That's what they left at the appointed place for Pauloosie to pick up and take to traders like Fox. Factories in Europe and Canada and America bought the down for insulation in quilts and pillows. Expensive quilts and pillows. A season's worth of down brought enough money for Idlouk to buy his flour and things like that for cooking and the batteries for his feather sterilizer and whatever else he needed. He could live all year on just that money.

Alvin's fingers moved swiftly now; practice had made him good at this. And he realized with surprise that he hadn't written to Mamma and Grandma about this job yet. He'd talked about the feathers as though they understood it all. Well, he would explain—in his very next letter. He'd tell Mamma he was earning his way. Idlouk said he had never wanted a helper before, but now that he had one, he was glad. Alvin would tell Mamma and Grandma that. They could be proud of him. Sometimes when he went to sleep, he lay on his bedroll and just felt good for a long time. He'd tell them that, too.

Alvin carefully lifted the feathers from the bowl into the sterilizer and turned on the heat.

Idlouk put a hand on Alvin's shoulder. Alvin had

heard him come in even though Idlouk moved quietly. Idlouk checked the dial on the sterilizer but didn't say a word. So Alvin had done everything right.

"My traps were empty," said Idlouk. "Let's go check yours."

Alvin put on his gear, and they tramped along the trail in the snow that they had made a couple of days ago, when they set these traps. Alvin had set only one by himself, way off toward the east. They followed that side trail, and there it was, a hare, caught by one foot. Mercifully, it was dead and frozen. Alvin wasn't surprised: Trapped animals anywhere died of fear and shock all the time, but in the cold it happened faster. He reset the trap, and they went back home.

When they got inside, Idlouk built a lichen fire and Alvin set the hare on the floor in front of it. It was important to thaw it so that Idlouk wouldn't damage the hide when he skinned it. Idlouk needed that hide for a summer blanket he was making. Alvin turned the hare over and moved it closer to the heat.

Idlouk took out his *ulu*, a crescent-shaped knife that had belonged to his mother. Alvin moved close so that he could see everything perfectly. Idlouk was fast at skinning, and Alvin loved to watch him. But Idlouk handed the *ulu* to Alvin. "It's your catch."

Alvin's ears got all funny feeling. His catch. All he had done was set the trap, but this was his catch. This was what hunting meant. He'd been willing to set the trap—so he should be willing to deal with the prey. And he knew how to do this; he'd watched carefully so many times.

He handed the *ulu* back to Idlouk and took out his father's pocketknife instead. It might be harder to do the job this way, but this was Alvin's catch—he should skin it with this knife.

He lay the hare out long and smoothed its pure white coat gently, touching the black tips on the ears. He cut off the feet first, like Idlouk always did, working the blade through the joints cleanly. Next he cut the skin away from around the hare's mouth and eyes. He kept the knife sharp, so it cut easy. He laid the knife aside and pushed the skin back down over the head. The first time he had seen Idlouk do this, it had amazed him. It was as though the hare had on a ski mask and its head poked out through the mouth opening. He looked over his shoulder at Idlouk.

Idlouk handed Alvin a square of cloth.

Alvin wrapped the cloth around the skinless hare head and gripped the wrapped head with his left hand. Then he slid the fingers of his right hand between the skin and the flesh, reaching his right arm all the way down the spine to the tail. He hadn't expected the hide to separate from the flesh so easily; it was as though the hare hide was nothing more than a loose bodysuit.

He worked his hand around the tummy and down each of the four legs till every bit of hide was free from the flesh. Then he pulled out his arm. It was slick with mucus, but not bloody. He grabbed the scruff of the neck fur and yanked hard. But he wasn't holding the head of the hare firmly enough, and it slipped out of his hand. He rewrapped the head with the cloth and held it as tight as he could. Then he grabbed the neck fur again and yanked and yanked and yanked. Suddenly the skin just slipped away from the tail end. And there he was, with a skinned hare in one hand and an empty hide in the other.

And there was no blood anywhere.

Alvin grinned and held the hide out to Idlouk. "It'll be good in your blanket."

"It's yours, Kukukulik. Your first catch. If we lived with other people, we would call them all together now to eat your hare in a big celebration."

Alvin looked at the skinless hare in his left hand.

It seemed pathetically small. "There's barely enough here to feed you and me."

"That's okay. If we had ten people, everyone would take a big bite. If we had twenty, everyone would take a smaller bite."

"And if we had thirty, everyone would just take a whiff?" asked Alvin.

Idlouk laughed. "Shall we eat the hare for breakfast?"

"Yes. But since it's my catch, I get to choose—and I want it cooked."

Alvin spread the skin on the floor, to be cleaned later. They roasted the hare and ate it.

Alvin chewed extra long.

The duck feathers were sterilized by now, so Idlouk packed them in a bag, and the two of them picked debris from more feathers and refilled the sterilizer.

Idlouk turned his back on Alvin, and when he turned back again, he had a cloth spread over his hand. The guessing game.

Alvin reached under the cloth and felt carefully. Sharp bits. Stringy bits. Little parts fell off like dust as he touched, even though he was touching lightly. And, oh, here was something soft. He thought he recognized it, and shook his head in confusion. "Fur?"

"Good."

But what was all the other stuff? Alvin rolled something between his thumb and index finger. It was thin and about an inch long. Like part of a broken toothpick. Like a very small bone. "Is it a dead hare?"

Idlouk pulled the cloth off. In his hand was a brown tangled mess of rooty strands with white things stuck in it here and there. He poured it into Alvin's cupped hands. "Droppings from a snowy owl."

Alvin looked at his hands in dismay. He was holding bird droppings. "So these are the undigested parts of a hare?"

"A lemming and whatever else it ate."

Alvin thought of Mamma's face all shocked and of Grandma's nose all wrinkled. He thought of his friends at home, grossed out. And he thought of Hardette, who couldn't even deal with food that had dropped on the ground. He laughed. And the funniest thing of all was that it wasn't disgusting. It was interesting.

Idlouk stirred up the mess in Alvin's hands with one finger. He pulled out a mangled feather. "Do you recognize this?"

How could Alvin not? He worked with those feathers all the time. "An eider duck feather."

"Droppings tell you what animals have been where you are and how long ago. It's important to stop and check them."

"Won't you get a disease from touching them?"

"Any bacteria from the animal's intestines die in the cold," said Idlouk.

"What should I do with this?"

"Throw it in the fire."

Alvin wiped off his hands and stretched. "Can we go out now?"

They put on their gear and walked toward Mount Thule. They hadn't been outside more than fifteen minutes when the stars turned green, then pink, then every color, showering all around them, aurora bore-alis—the northern lights. The Inuit called it *arsaniit*. This was the heavenly display Alvin had seen that first day he came to Bylot Island. And even though he'd seen it lots since then, every time its glory made him dizzy. "This is the first aurora we've seen in days," he said.

"When the thaw comes," said Idlouk, "we'll hardly see it anymore."

Alvin stopped walking and turned in a circle slowly. This great wonder wouldn't be his day after day—it would disappear. He vowed to give it his full attention each time it happened from now on, just like Ms. Artiga always said—full attention. He'd give his full attention to cleaning feathers and skinning animals and examining droppings. He'd give his full attention to everything, and there was so much of everything to give his attention to.

He spun in a circle of gratitude.

CHAPTER TWENTY-SEVEN

White and Black

The waves were gigantic. Idlouk and Alvin stood on a cliff and watched the bright emerald peaks of water. A storm was coming for sure. The air was so electric, Alvin felt a buzz in his teeth.

"Let's get home." Idlouk led the way, poking the snow with his walking pole.

The snow came softly at first, but within minutes it was coming down fast and heavy. The whole world was white. Alvin could hardly see. He stayed close behind Idlouk.

Alvin had been in two storms already, and he knew that if you watched the drifting snow you'd be able to

tell the directions and find your way home, because
the wind came from the north. Even when there
wasn't a storm, you could tell the directions from the
hardened drifts of past winds. But this wind was different. It kept changing directions.

Idlouk changed directions too. And not in a
normal way. He was wandering. Alvin realized that
Idlouk was lost. They were lost in a blizzard! It was
impossible to see the hardened drifts. It was
impossible to see anything.

Idlouk stopped and whacked at the snow with his
arm coming down like a machete knife. Immediately
Alvin knew what he was doing; after all, Alvin had
helped build igloos on his trip to Pond Inlet with
Oodlateeta and Akkavak. Alvin whacked too. In less
than a half hour, they sat inside the igloo and listened to the shrieks of the wild winds.

It was completely black inside the igloo. Alvin felt
like he had traveled to the very end of the earth. And
beyond, out into deep space.

Soon the heat from their bodies melted the
cracks in the snow, sealing the walls of the igloo. It
got warm. Alvin knew it would, but still he had to
marvel at a warm home made of snow. He laughed.

"When my grandfather was young," said Idlouk,

"the Inuit on Greenland went out in their boats even in blizzards." His voice resonated in the igloo and gave the eerie sense that he was millions of miles away. "The boats were called *umiaks,* and they were made of walrus skin over a whalebone or driftwood frame. They held several men, who poled and hauled the *umiaks* through cracks in the ice."

Alvin hugged his knees against his chest. "I wouldn't go out on the sea in a blizzard. I wouldn't go out even in a normal storm."

"You might have, if you'd grown up with everyone around you doing it."

Alvin didn't think so. Matthew Henson probably would have. But not Alvin. "Did you ever ride in an *umiak*?"

"Sure. But you can't. No one in Greenland uses *umiaks* anymore. No one anywhere uses them."

"Because kayaks are better?"

"Kayaks are small. *Umiaks* could carry a whole family and everything they owned," said Idlouk. "No, people just stopped using them. I don't know why. Lots of the old ways have been lost."

"You still follow the old ways."

"Only some of them. The Inuit were nomadic people. If I followed the old ways, I'd have gone south for the winter, right behind the caribou."

"Why don't you do that?"

"The government would give me trouble. People aren't allowed to live like I live anymore. In the 1960s the Inuit were forced into government-built towns. Some of them still hunt. But the old ways are dying." Idlouk's voice was flat—not even tinged with sadness. As though everything he cared about had already died long ago. And that was sadder than if Idlouk had cried.

Alvin scooched toward Idlouk till their *kamiks* touched. "Some people are trying to bring the old ways back. They're teaching the old ways to people who committed crimes."

"I know about that. Pauloosie brings me newspapers now and then. It's a good idea. But it might be too late."

The noise of the wind grew louder.

"The wind scares me," said Alvin.

"The wind scares everyone," said Idlouk.

Alvin dropped his forehead on his knees. They sat silent, lost in the black, the noise of the wind whipping outside. The scent of their hair and breath and sweat made the air pungent.

Suddenly Alvin remembered the humpback whale that had swum by the day before. They had seen the spray of the blow and run toward the sea for a better look. But it went under and all they could see was the tail. Still, Idlouk knew it was a humpback because it went straight down.

Alvin wondered if it was alone, if it was a scout for its pod, checking out whether spring was here yet. He worried about it. Whales breathe air—so that meant whales can drown. "I hope that humpback whale doesn't have trouble in the blizzard."

"He was adult; he's got experience." But Idlouk didn't say anything else. No promise of safety.

Alvin was grateful for that. Idlouk was always honest with him. He pressed his head hard against his knees. "I want that whale to live and have a baby and play with it in the sound."

"Ah," said Idlouk loudly. "Sometimes in summer I take a whole afternoon off from work and just watch the whale families play."

Alvin smiled, though Idlouk couldn't see him. Then he missed Mamma and Grandma. He always missed them. But now he missed them even more.

Alvin woke from the ache of hunger. Instantly the quiet told him the blizzard was over. He stretched. Every part of him was stiff.

Idlouk banged around. At first Alvin didn't know what he was doing, then snow fell on his head and a ray of light came in. Idlouk had punched a hole through the layer of snow over the breathing hole in the top of the igloo. Together they cut their way out. The wind was still blowing, but it was an ordinary wind now. They tramped home in bright sunshine.

"Hungry?" said Idlouk.

"I'll make us cookies," Alvin said.

"I'll go check the traps."

"But don't you want to rest a while?"

"We slept for a day," said Idlouk. "I need to walk. And we deserve a little feast after all that." He left.

Alvin built a fire in the stone stove and made a batch of cookies. He was expert at it. It took almost no time at all. Then he sat down and wrote a letter to Mamma and Grandma. When he finished, Idlouk still wasn't back.

And now he realized Idlouk was right; Alvin needed a walk too. At least inside Idlouk's home they could get up and move around. But inside the igloo they'd stayed in one position for hours.

He grabbed his walking pole and went outside. He wouldn't go far. He'd never gone far without Idlouk at his side. He headed toward the cliffs, but within ten minutes or so, the winds suddenly picked up again. And they were crazy, like yesterday, as though the blizzard had simply taken a little rest and now was back in full force. The sky dumped buckets of snow.

Alvin ran back toward home. He raced against the snow, his heart thumping in his head. And then the snow blinded him, like he knew it would. He screamed to Idlouk, but snow filled his mouth.

His brain stopped and for a moment the only thing he was aware of was how hard it was just to breathe with the wind stealing the air from him. It knocked him off his feet.

Then thoughts came again. He couldn't be that far from the tunnel at their front door, but he didn't know which way to go.

He was scared to move. If he went the wrong way, he'd be lost in the snow and Idlouk would never find him. His face was freezing. He had on his parka and breeches, but he hadn't wrapped his scarf around his nose because he hadn't planned to go far.

The snow was piling up fast. Alvin couldn't just stay there on all fours. So he crawled. He crawled in bigger and bigger circles. Round and around. It felt like forever.

His head hit something solid. He nearly wept from relief. It was the tunnel to their front door. Alvin crawled through.

Idlouk wasn't there.

Alvin lit the oil lamp and watched the little flame flicker.

The winds were deafening.

Alvin paced.

Finally Idlouk crawled through the front door.

Alvin ran to him and hugged him, even though he was covered with snow.

"We caught two hares," said Idlouk. "But I lost them both in the storm."

"That's okay," said Alvin. "A wolf will find them and be happy. Have a cookie."

So they ate cookies and played music and told stories. Idlouk said Alvin was smart for crawling in circles. Alvin listened with pride—and a touch of fear. He'd done the right thing, but he didn't really know how the idea came to him. He remembered Manitok in the train station in Churchill saying someone somewhere was on Alvin's side.

CHAPTER TWENTY-EIGHT

The Last Long Letter

Dear Mamma and Grandma,

The animals are changing with the daylight. For a while, the sun lasted a little longer each day. But then it started lasting a lot longer. Now the sun rises early and shines hard till late at night. The walruses are all over the inlet; they roar and bellow day and night. The slushy snow barely holds the wide hoofprints of the caribou that are coming back. We can hear their hoofbeats from miles away, the herds are so big.

A few days ago we came across a pile of stones. It turned out to be an old trap. Idlouk called it by the Greenland name, *ullisautit,* because he doesn't know how the Inuit in Pond Inlet call it. They're like stone igloos with no entrance, but a hole at the top. The Inuit who used to live here would put bait on a piece of hide stretched over the hole. When the animal went for the bait, it fell into the hole and couldn't get out. They used them mostly for trapping foxes. But this one was huge, and Idlouk bet it was for trapping polar bears.

And, oh, you're going to love this: Yesterday I spied newborn seals in the snow tunnels their mothers had dug. They were fat and short, and three of them were sleeping. But one flopped around when I peeked into his tunnel.

It was easy to get close. I just did what the Inuit do when they hunt—I moved quietly and acted like a seal. I can see a lot when I'm quiet, because the animals don't run off and hide. And it feels right to be quiet. It's like you always tell me to be polite—well, being quiet feels polite here.

I can still see white in most directions, but I know the snow will be gone soon. It's funny how used to it I am. I bet I'll never feel cold in Washington again.

Our days are busy now. It's like we're coming out of hibernation, Idlouk and me. We have so much work to do. That's why I'm not going to write long letters anymore. It takes a lot of time to write like this—too much. I work mostly outside now. And when I'm inside, I want to eat and sleep. So, instead, I'll just write you short notes. Just what we did, so I can remember later—not what I think about it all.

You're not getting the letters anyway. So I guess I wasn't really writing them for you. Or not totally for you. I think maybe I wrote long things to feel like I wasn't so far away. I pretended I was talking to you. But I am far away. I really am. And that's okay. This is my home for now. When I come back to you, I'll tell you everything in person. Well, not everything—not the things that will make you cry.

I love you. And I talk to you in my head as I'm walking around outside. I'll tell you all my thoughts there. So listen to the words in my head, sweet Mamma, sweet Grandma. And one day you'll hear them for real.

'Cause I'm going to come back alive. I hope you know that. I won't die someplace where you don't even know where I am. I won't do that to you.

Love,

Alvin

CHAPTER TWENTY-NINE

Ducks

Spring came late to Bylot Island. Alvin ran around the outside of the house in his sweatsuit and *kamiks* and laughed at the pure joy of being able to move freely, unencumbered by parka and breeches. Then he ran back inside till the shivers subsided. The snow was melting fast. On the uncovered patches of tundra purple lupines and yellow buttercups sprouted. Idlouk said the Inuit loved this time of year. They called it *upirngaaq*.

Alvin and Idlouk didn't trap anymore. Idlouk wouldn't kill a land animal in its mating season. So they hunted, and only if they thought an animal was too old to mate would they kill it. Animals were returning from the south every day, so hunting was a quick chore. They ate old goose, which was gamey and good, and so many kinds of fish. Spring fishing was one of Idlouk's favorite activities.

What took more time was keeping records of the birds they saw. Idlouk knew everything about the birds, and he was teaching Alvin. So far Alvin had recorded the sightings of thirty different species. Idlouk had logs that went back decades, with each day numbered—one for the day of the first sighting of a returning bird species, then on from there. Alvin leafed through them, marveling at the regularity of the order in which the different species returned. One day they spotted a barn swallow, then a few days later a robin. Idlouk worried because those species had never traveled so far north before. Global warming was changing things.

Alvin hiked with Idlouk at least an hour every day with binoculars, sighting the birds. He loved best the murres, which looked a lot like puffins. They dove underwater and disappeared for so long he was always just about sure they'd drowned, but up they'd pop again, fish flopping in those thick bills. And he loved the kittiwakes, the small gulls that flocked on the cliffs.

And, of course, he loved the greater snow geese.

But Alvin and Idlouk's main activity involved only one type of bird: the eider duck.

In the mornings they visited the ducks. Idlouk loaded his canvas rucksack with dozens of yellow wooden pegs, a plastic bag, Magic Markers, hammers, a thermos of tea—he loved tea as much as Oodlateeta and Grandma did—and Alvin's cookies. That way they could wander for hours before having to return home for a hot meal.

They walked through the snow, with Alvin behind Idlouk, stepping only where Idlouk had already gone, until they got to the ridge that ran along the south of the island. But once they hit that ridge, they could walk side by side because that was the first part of the island to become free of snow. And that's why it was the first nesting area claimed by the ducks. The nests sat in shallow scrapes out in the open. As Alvin and Idlouk approached, the ridge looked speckled with white and black—the drakes. The females, mottled brown, sat on their nests.

This morning they had gotten up early and eaten a hearty breakfast of caribou sitting on the floor of the house. Idlouk said it was traditional to sit on the floor when you ate from a large carcass. He loved tradition. He loved anything he had learned from his grandfather.

Alvin got dressed and pulled his hat on. Idlouk had taught him to twist his hair at night so that it would form thick clumps and make his hat fit. It worked; the hat was snug. So Mamma didn't buy it too big, after all.

They walked in their customary silence outdoors. They had spent most of their waking hours and all of their sleeping hours together for months. By now they understood each other in that quiet, weighted way that Idlouk had slowly taught Alvin.

A female eider duck spotted them and burst from her nest in a panic. She flew out toward the open water. Idlouk kneeled by that nest and began his job.

Alvin walked boldly toward the next nest. The duck flapped away and Alvin got to work. First he took a peg from Idlouk's rucksack, kneeled beside the nest, and wrote 1.4 on the peg with the Magic Marker. He hammered the peg into the ground about three feet from the nest. The 1 meant that this was the first time that season that they'd visited that nest. The 4 meant that there were four eggs in the nest. They never visited a nest a second time until all the nests had been visited at least once. And twice was the most Idlouk ever visited a nest in a season.

Alvin inspected the nest carefully. It was full of down that the female had plucked from her chest. There was more than enough there to cushion these eggs and protect them from the cold. Idlouk claimed that eiderdown was the best insulation in the world. Alvin took a handful, careful to leave plenty on top of the warm eggs.

Quack!

Alvin stepped away quickly. He tucked his head to his chest and clasped his hands behind his neck, to protect himself from the mother bird. But the dive-bomb didn't come. Alvin looked around. The duck belonged to a different nest. She stood in front of it and flapped her wings threateningly and quacked loud.

"It won't hurt the eggs," Alvin told her. "I promise."

But the mother duck quacked even louder and stepped toward him.

He gathered the feathers he had dropped at the first quack and stuffed them into the plastic bag in the rucksack. Then he moved off to a nest far from the protective mother duck and got to work again.

They would collect feathers all spring, clean the down, sterilize it, and bag it for Pauloosie to pick up every week at the drop-off point. But they couldn't clean it nearly as fast as they could collect it. So a lot of it was packed away to be cleaned during the rest of the year, when the world froze again, just like they'd been doing since Alvin arrived.

This morning they went from nest to nest for hours. Finally Idlouk leaned his rifle against a rock and took out the thermos and cookies.

Alvin had never seen Idlouk shoot, even though he carried the rifle all the time these days. "What's the rifle for?"

"Polar bears. Soon there will be more than a hundred on Bylot."

Alvin knew the polar bears would return after the caribou—but a hundred of them! And so soon. "I thought you said they wouldn't be back till summer."

"It's late May—almost June."

Already? This wasn't spring—it was practically summer. An Arctic summer. The sunlight hadn't speeded up, it had come at its usual incremental rate—but Alvin had lost track of time. May. Late May.

May in Washington, D.C., could be cool and bright or hot and muggy. Was Mamma wearing shorts on the job yet? Had she survived poison ivy season without a rash? Rock Creek Park teemed with it. Alvin remembered Mother's Day last year; he'd given her a tube of hydrocortisone for her poison ivy and a gallon of chocolate chip ice cream. And she'd given Grandma bananas, chocolate chips, walnuts, and Hershey syrup. They'd had banana splits for lunch.

Late May.

Mamma and Grandma hadn't heard from Alvin in nearly half a year. And he hadn't heard from them. Anything could have happened.

Alvin munched on a cookie and moved closer to Idlouk. The rifle leaned between them. "Does it have bullets or blanks?"

"Bullets."

Bullets and polar bears. A little spasm shot through Alvin's shoulders.

The air filled with the *coo-rho, coo-rho* cries of the courting eider ducks. He looked over the sparkling sea and watched a group of ducks go by on an ice floe.

"Soon the sun will shine all the time," said Alvin. He thought about that a moment and got confused. "Does that mean it just goes back and forth across the sky?"

"No. It makes a circular path."

"Wow." Alvin smiled. "Amazing."

"And the mosquitoes will swarm," said Idlouk.

"Really? Insects come this far north?"

"They're always here," said Idlouk. "They make it through the winter with a special liquid inside, sort of like car antifreeze."

Alvin laughed. "What else don't I know?"

"There are no reptiles in the Arctic."

"Wow. What else?"

"All sorts of things. Want to climb an iceberg?"

"What?"

"This was an easy winter. The ice in Baffin Bay is already breaking up, and it's loaded with icebergs."

"Can we really climb them?"

"It's tricky. But it's also beautiful."

"Let's go," said Alvin.

"Home first. We have to drop off all this stuff."

Once they had put away the rucksack and the feathers, they headed out again. Idlouk led the way, of course, poking the patches of snow with his walking pole.

The sunshine felt wonderful, and Alvin trudged along with his hood down. He let Idlouk get far ahead so that he could enjoy being alone. He was wearing his old gloves, not his big mittens, but he took them off, just like Idlouk did, and swung his arms as best he could in his parka.

The sky was the cleanest, clearest blue he could imagine. The sea was a minty green with chunks of ice floes. And out near the center of the bay the water changed to jade green. A snow goose with powerful black-tipped wings flew by, all alone. But Alvin could hear the rest of the flock honking in the distance.

There were no houses, no buildings of any sort, as far as he could see. There were no boats on the sea. Idlouk had told him that a supply ship came once every summer to Pond Inlet. Maybe the ship would come early this year, because of the easy winter. He scanned the horizon. Sea. Never-ending sea.

The only things that truly seemed to exist in this moment were the birds of the sky and the plants that peeked out of the half-thawed ground here and there. This is what it must have been like to walk the earth thousands of years ago.

Alvin felt complete and wild. Had Mamma ever had such a taste of the wild?

Mamma and Grandma.

What would they do if they could see him now?

Would they be overwhelmed with the hugeness and starkness of this life?

But Alvin was beginning to understand it. He was mindful of the immensity of nature—respectful of the way the world could change, fast and without warning—especially the weather. But he walked with confidence. And he was happy. Deeply happy.

They'd been walking only about ten minutes when Alvin saw Idlouk fall through the snow up to his chest. His arms stretched out to both sides on top of the snow with the rifle in his left hand. The walking pole had been flung aside.

Alvin came running from behind.

"Stop!" hissed Idlouk. "Don't come near. Don't speak over a whisper."

Alvin circled Idlouk, giving him wide berth, until he faced him. "What happened?" he whispered back.

Fear transfigured Idlouk's face. Idlouk knew something Alvin didn't know. What? Was this some strange kind of snow, like quicksand, pulling him under? He'd never seen Idlouk afraid before. He hadn't thought it was possible.

Idlouk whispered, "Don't make me talk more than I have to. Try to find a way to pull me out. Fast. But you can't come close. And test with the walking pole before you step anywhere."

A way to pull him out. They had no gear with them, nothing except the rifle in Idlouk's hand. And the walking pole wasn't sturdy enough for that kind of job.

Alvin stripped off his parka and breeches and ran home, sticking to the path they came on, so that he didn't need to use the walking pole. He grabbed the rope. But Idlouk was so much larger than Alvin. Alvin would never be able to support Idlouk's weight. What could he fasten the other end of the rope to? There were no rocks near where Idlouk fell.

Alvin's eyes passed the rucksack. Pegs! He grabbed the rucksack and ran.

The whole thing had taken him less than a quarter hour, he'd gone so fast. Idlouk was exactly as Alvin had left him, except his head was tilted backward so that he looked at the sky and both hands were bent upward at the wrist so that they didn't touch the snow at all. His rifle was still in his left hand, hovering above the snow. Alvin tossed the rope. The end of it landed in front of Idlouk's chest. And the snow caved a little. The snow caved from the slap of the rope! What was going on?

"I can't reach it," Idlouk mouthed. "If I move, I'll fall all the way."

All the way where? Wasn't there any ground under that snow? Terror squeezed Alvin's heart. He had trouble seeing. Idlouk was a blur.

And now he knew why Idlouk had tilted his head back and bent his hands upward: To keep his heat off the snow. His parka kept his body heat inside, but his breath and hands were culprits. Oh, Lord.

Alvin took out a bunch of pegs and tapped them into the ground, being as quiet and fast as he could. He placed each peg just a hand span from the last. Then he wove his end of the rope in and out of the pegs tightly, so the rope would stay. He left a tail to hold onto.

The sun on the snow dazzled him. He felt disoriented and strange. How many seconds was this taking? A laugh threatened to bubble up. Alvin realized he was getting giddy, almost hysterical. He swallowed and turned back to Idlouk. He wanted Idlouk to tell him that he'd done the right thing, that it would work. He wanted to hear Idlouk's low voice steadying him, guiding him, as it had through so many new tasks. But Idlouk didn't move. Alvin wanted to scream to Idlouk to talk, to move, to make it all right again.

He had to control himself.

He concentrated on the distant honks of the snow geese as he sat down and dug in his heels, with the pegs between him and Idlouk. He wrapped his end of the rope around his left hand, gripping hard. He gently pulled the other end of the rope back toward him. Then he tossed the free end again, this time precisely onto Idlouk's right hand, and instantly grabbed his own end of the rope with both hands.

And the snow gave way. All of it. In a huge circle centered on Idlouk. And Idlouk was falling.

He heard Idlouk's little cry of pain as he slammed up against the side of the abyss. He heard the smack of the rifle hitting somewhere deep below. From where Alvin was, he couldn't see Idlouk at all, but he could see the emptiness beyond him. It was at least a fifty-foot drop, with rocky points sticking up at the bottom.

Alvin held on to his end of the rope with all his might. He didn't feel any of Idlouk's weight yet, because the pegs were holding firm. If only they would keep holding. His ears buzzed and his tears fell.

He was sure Idlouk was doomed, dangling there. But then he saw jerks on the rope. Idlouk must be climbing it. Alvin imagined Idlouk's hands, inching up the rope, the left one always under the right one. Or was he climbing hand over hand? That would have been faster. But he was an old man. And his hands were gnarled.

A peg popped from the ground and the rope slipped just that much more into the hole. But the jerks came faster now. Maybe Idlouk's feet had found ledges and he was using them to climb out. Oh, yes, that had to be it. He had to climb fast. Please.

Another peg popped.

"Hurry, Idlouk!" screamed Alvin. He pulled against the force of the rope, staying as low to the ground as he could so he wouldn't pull the pegs up.

Another peg popped.

Alvin counted the remaining pegs. Seven. Seven pegs and then he would be supporting Idlouk's weight all by himself.

Idlouk's right hand appeared on the rope over the edge of the hole.

Another peg popped.

Idlouk's hand slipped out of sight.

"Hurry!" he screamed again.

And there was Idlouk's right hand once more. And his left. And now his whole right arm.

Pop, pop, pop. The pegs came out of the ground one after the other.

Alvin pulled with every ounce of strength he had. He fell to his back just as Idlouk's chest lunged onto the ground.

Alvin scrambled to his feet and grabbed Idlouk under each arm. He lugged at him, even though Idlouk was now clearly safe. He kept lugging until Idlouk got to his knees on the solid ground. And now Idlouk was on his feet, and Alvin stood tight in the circle of Idlouk's arms.

They stumbled away from the edge and sat, clutching each other. When Alvin finally stopped shaking and pulled away, Idlouk pointed into the deep hole. "The snow often freezes over gaps on this part of the island," he said. "I poked with my pole and I thought I'd hit solid ground, but it must have been a freak ice formation."

So that's what Pauloosie had meant when he'd given Alvin his walking pole so long ago and told him that if he didn't feel firm ground, he should go another way. Alvin had lived here all this time and never known how important Idlouk's rule was about following him in the snow, about stepping only where he had stepped. He felt aghast at his dumb luck.

They got to their feet again slowly and went home.

Alvin expected them to stay there. But Idlouk told Alvin to put on his parka and breeches. He grabbed his old extra rifle and walked right back out toward the iceberg. This time, though, they walked the tundra from bare patch to bare patch, avoiding the larger stretches of open snow.

They went in silence for a while, just like before. Then Idlouk whistled. His whistle sliced through the cold sunshine. It sounded awful, but it helped Alvin anyhow. Idlouk was whistling "What a Wonderful World."

"Idlouk, did you whistle that before?"

"What do you mean?"

"Do you whistle it at night or something, like when I'm sleeping?"

"I haven't whistled in years, Kukukulik." Idlouk laughed. "Can't you tell? I only whistled now because I know how much you love Louis Armstrong and I know how scared you were."

"But I remember a man whistling. Whistling that song. And he whistled bad, just like you."

"What man?" asked Idlouk.

And Alvin knew. "My father."

"Did he love Louis Armstrong as much as you?"

"I don't know. I thought I didn't remember him

till just a second ago. But that whistle is in my head. And I can remember sitting on his shoulders now, holding on to his forehead, hanging my head backward like you did in that hole, and staring up at the night sky, bouncing to the rhythm of that whistle." Alvin smiled with warm realization. "He must have loved Louis Armstrong. My uncle Pete said he loved jazz and the blues. I bet my father whistled all the time."

"If he whistled as bad as me, I'm sorry for your mother."

Alvin stared at him. "How can you joke like that? Half an hour ago you could have died."

"I will die," said Idlouk. "But I think not today."

"What would you have done if I hadn't been there?" asked Alvin.

"I'd have waited as still as I could until night, when the temperature drops and the snow becomes more rigid. Then I would have tried to work my way out onto the crust of snow."

"Could you have done it?"

"I doubt it."

Alvin hated Idlouk's words; he hated that truth. But that's how life was. Idlouk had needed Alvin, even though Alvin was a kid. People simply needed one another. He thought of Mamma and Grandma—they needed him, too. It wasn't just that they loved him. They needed him. "Idlouk?"

"What, Kukukulik?"

"You were afraid. I saw it in your face." Alvin shuddered at the memory.

"Look at the sea."

Alvin looked hard. "There's nothing there."

"That's right. Sometimes you see the blow of whales. But today you just see forever." Idlouk smiled. "That's beauty."

Alvin remembered Hardette's words when she'd sat across from him in the dining car and tried to guess at why he was traveling north. She talked about the beauty of the journey. And he remembered how Matthew Henson loved the fierce beauty of the Arctic. But Idlouk wasn't on a journey, and he wasn't an explorer. He lived here all alone. "Why did you come here in the first place, Idlouk? Why did you leave people?"

"I didn't leave people; I didn't have anyone to leave. My wife died. We had no children. My only brother moved to Denmark years before."

"But you left society. Don't you miss that?"

"A part of me always connected best with the outdoors. With the birds. The smells in the air. I belong here. Not everyone does"—Idlouk glanced at Alvin—"but I do." His stride lengthened.

Alvin kept up with Idlouk, his eyes on the mossy rocks here and there. Then he stopped. "Idlouk, I need to talk."

Idlouk pointed. "Look."

The iceberg stood majestic before them, surrounded on three sides by water.

"Can it hold till tonight?" asked Idlouk.

Alvin nodded.

"Then we'll talk tonight."

Alvin quickly learned that climbing an iceberg didn't mean climbing to the top. The top is a tower of glare ice and no one climbs up it. Climbing an iceberg meant walking across frozen sea and climbing onto it and walking around the edges and sitting and looking out over the water.

On another iceberg he saw a creamy seal pup, about four feet long, lying half on ice, half in water, basking in the sun. An adult seal came up behind it and playfully splashed water on its face. The pup slid off the ice and dove after the mother.

A loud crack shook Alvin to the core. He jumped up. "What was that?"

"The spirit of the iceberg." Idlouk smiled.

"It sounded like thunder." Alvin sat down beside Idlouk again. "You really think the iceberg has a spirit?"

"Everyone and everything has a spirit, Kukukulik."

Alvin watched the seals play in the frigid water.

When they were walking home, he kept thinking of the clutter and noise and abandon of a Mount Pleasant late-spring afternoon. He thought of the chalk drawings the kids did on the sidewalks. The smells of gingerbread and chocolate from Heller's Bakery. The screech of the bus brakes at the triangle of grass on Mount Pleasant Street. He thought of Mamma's smooth cheeks and Grandma's soft, sagging ones. He thought of Shastri.

That night Alvin and Idlouk played the game Alvin loved best. Alvin felt under the cloth and laughed. It was an egg. But guessing an egg wasn't enough, of course. He had to guess the kind. This egg was larger than a gull's and smoother than a great snowy owl's and rounder than a goose's. He rolled it in his hands. He guessed it was an auk egg. And he was right.

Immediately exhaustion overcame him. His bones

felt rubbery; his muscles weary. He climbed into his bedroll and stared into the dark. He heard Idlouk's soft coughs as he stoked the fire. Alvin rolled onto his side. Idlouk was lying on his belly on the floor, blowing into the flames.

Alvin sat up. "Idlouk?"

"Yes, Kukukulik."

"I'm going home."

"I thought that's what you were going to say." Idlouk sat on the edge of the platform. He picked up his old rifle, which glistened from the oiling he'd given it when they got home, and rubbed the barrel with a hare hide. When he looked at Alvin, his eyes were red and his face was streaked with tears from blowing into the fire. He looked older than anyone on Earth could possibly be. Alvin felt a protective urge—Idlouk needed him. But then Idlouk smiled, strong and reliable. "You're ready."

Alvin was surprised. "What do you mean?"

"You've grown."

Alvin looked down at his legs. They did seem longer. And they were thick with muscles from hiking through snow. He wasn't Dwarf anymore. He wasn't that drug dealer's idea of a perfect runner.

He felt his hair—it was short and tight when he

left home in January. Now his fingers got lost in the thick, long, bushy tangle that had formed from trying to make his hat fit. "I wish I could see myself in a mirror."

"I wasn't talking about your body. Your spirit has grown. You're free."

Free. That's what Alvin had longed to be. That was it exactly.

He snuggled his hands under his bottom and sat on them as he watched the fire leap in strange shapes. "I'll miss everything here. The caribou and the walrus and the musk oxen. The huge sky and the water. I'll miss you, Idlouk." He moved closer to Idlouk. "Come with me. You're too old to stay alone."

Idlouk rubbed the rifle stock now. "I don't want to leave."

"Please, I want you with me."

"I'll be with you, Kukukulik."

"How?"

"Think of me."

Alvin smiled. "You know what, Idlouk? You would love my grandma."

CHAPTER THIRTY

Home

Pauloosie stood beside the two-man kayak and held it in place while Alvin climbed on board. Idlouk loaded bags of down into the kayak in silence. On both sides of them, the little plants that had been simple green only a few days ago were now covered in brilliant pink saxifrage blossoms.

Idlouk picked a blossom. He went on picking until he had a full bouquet. Then he stuck it in one of the plastic bags he always carried for duck down and handed it to Pauloosie, who climbed into the boat and gave it to Alvin.

Pauloosie paddled across the sound. Alvin

remembered shuffling along here in mid-February. Everything was completely different now. The sound wouldn't be crossable by foot again until late November.

Alvin waved good-bye to Idlouk. Idlouk waved, the new rifle under one arm and Alvin's pennywhistle in his hand. Then he put it to his lips, turned, and walked away. The high, familiar song transfixed Alvin. "Good-bye," shouted Alvin suddenly. "Good-bye, good-bye." Idlouk stopped and waved again.

That's it, thought Alvin—*taima*—the end. He was sad. But it was time.

He looked ahead. The boat rocked with each move of the paddle, and Alvin remembered that man and woman who drowned off of Baffin Island years ago. But he wasn't afraid. The boat felt stable. Pauloosie obviously knew what he was doing. That was the trick— you could do just about anything if you worked hard and learned how. That was the trick to life.

That, and luck.

From the boat Alvin could see the outskirts of Pond Inlet. The huge garbage heap that had been frozen last time he saw it was now covered with scavenging birds. The gray ship in the harbor flew the Canadian flag— a maple leaf flapping in the wind. They went directly to the dock. Pauloosie and Alvin hugged each other in silence. Then Alvin climbed on board the Canadian supply ship.

Idlouk had paid for his tickets all the way home. As a twelve-year-old, Alvin could make the journey alone, as long as Idlouk paid adult fare for him. The ticket salesman even said that people would look out for Alvin on the boat and then on the various trains. Idlouk gave him spending money, too. He said Alvin had earned it, from all the work he'd done gathering and cleaning down.

Alvin gave Idlouk all the money he had brought with him—close to two hundred dollars—as payment for his room and board. It paid for almost a third of that new rifle.

It was funny to exchange money like that. Money was just money. But somehow it was important that the money that went into Idlouk's rifle came directly from Alvin's pocket. Every time Idlouk used that rifle, Alvin would be helping protect him even when he wasn't there.

The ship stayed docked at Pond Inlet for the rest of the day. Word must have gotten round that Alvin was on board, because by evening, a small group of towns-people had gathered on the shore. Only a few people spoke English, which was fine with Alvin, because he didn't feel like talking. After all these months in isolation with Idlouk, too much talk seemed like an intrusion. So he just waved and the people waved back. It was as though he was a celebrity. The boy who came to the Arctic and survived.

Not just survived. Alvin thought about all the new things he'd done, and he smiled. His father would have been proud of him.

He alternated between sleeping and practicing whistling all the way to Pangnirtung. Once when he woke, he saw a school of killer whales so close he could have hit them with a slingshot. The gulls flew above the boat and screamed out at the whales. When one of the crew members told him that the whales were after the baby seals that filled the waters these days, Alvin screamed at the whales too. Then he went back to his cabin and slept.

But as soon as the ship docked at Pangnirtung, he was off the boat and running. All the houses were drab gray shingles, now that he saw them without the snow cover—nothing like the colorful houses of Churchill. But he found the home he was looking for easily. No one was there except the two little girls, barefoot now, jumping on the furniture. No Oodlateeta, no Aima, no Fox. He left a dozen bear cookies for the little girls and a note that Oodlateeta and Aima, of course, could not read, but that Fox could translate for them later. He wrote, "Thank you. Thank you so much."

So many people had been generous with Alvin. So many strangers. He stared at the spectacular backdrop of mountains behind Pangnirtung, mountains he hadn't even seen in the dark of January, and he called out thanks—he called out *qujannamik*.

When the ship finally docked at Churchill, a man walked Alvin to the train station. But Manitok wasn't there. So Alvin left the parka, breeches, mittens, and *kamiks* that he'd taken, rolled up and tied with a rope. He tucked under the rope a sling he'd made—an *illuuk*—for hunting small animals. It was Tuesday, and the train for Winnipeg was to leave that night. Alvin sat in the train station, hoping Manitok would appear, but only the driver of the tourist bus appeared.

"Hello, Pete!" The bus driver gave him a big smile and a slap on the back.

Alvin smiled back. "You recognized me right away," he said with surprise.

"You are the only black person who comes to Churchill," said the bus driver.

Alvin gave a hooting whistle and laughed.

Then he got on board the train, put his pack under his seat, and fell asleep again.

The next few days he spent a lot of time reading the bird logs that Idlouk had given him as a parting gift. That's when he had given Idlouk the pennywhistle. He'd intended to all along, but that was the right moment.

When his eyes got tired from reading, he looked out the window at the Canadian expanses and he cupped his hands around his mouth and whistled softly, so he wouldn't disturb anyone. He bought sandwiches in the little stations they stopped at, and dozed on and off.

He had mailed his whole notebook of letters to Mamma and Grandma on the postal-service plane that left from Pond Inlet the day before he got on the ship, along with a final letter telling them he was coming home. They would arrive before him for sure. In his backpack was a long box filled with three bird nests: an eider duck's, an auk's, and a ptarmigan's. For Mamma. And the hide from that first hare he'd skinned. For Grandma.

He changed trains in Winnipeg without a problem. Then again in Toronto. He rode south out of Canada, south to New York, then boarded another train to Washington.

He had lost track of the days by the time he arrived in Washington's Union Station. But it was afternoon, he knew that much. He bought a Metro ticket for the closest stop, the one at the Zoo on Connecticut Avenue. He got out and walked slowly through the crowded zoo. Mount Pleasant lay on the other side. It had to be Saturday or Sunday, with all those school-age kids everywhere, because it wasn't late enough in June for the school year to have ended yet. So Mamma was probably home.

Alvin stopped by the polar bear pool and lingered, watching the huge dingy-coated animal paddle listlessly under water.

A teenage girl stood on the path behind him, hesitating, as though she was waiting for Alvin to leave before she'd come up to the pool. Alvin could almost smell her anxiety. He was taller than her, and a lot stronger, he was sure.

He moved a little to one side and smiled right at her.

She pushed her light brown hair back around her ears with both hands at once. Then she gave a quick smile and came up to the pool.

They stood side by side, watching the bear.

"He seems pathetic," said the girl at last. "They should throw some ice in his water."

An iceberg is more like it, thought Alvin. He closed his eyes against the enormity of what this bear was missing. Then he opened his eyes, smiled at the girl again, and waved good-bye.

She must have been Hardette's age. Tonight, after everything had calmed down, Alvin would call information in Winnipeg and ask for the Latimer family. He'd keep his promise to Hardette. Maybe they could start writing. Alvin had liked writing those letters to Mamma and Grandma all winter. It would be fun to get letters in return. And maybe next Kwanzaa, Hardette could visit Alvin, too, not just her New York cousins.

Or maybe they could meet in New York. Yes, that was it. He could earn money the rest of the summer and all fall, and he could take Mamma and Grandma to New York to see dancing on the stage. Alvin Ailey's company, or someone else just as great that Mamma would love. And he'd invite Hardette. It would be perfect

Alvin came out on the far side of the zoo, the Mount Pleasant side, and walked up the familiar blocks of his neighborhood. He listened to the cry of the gibbons behind him. They were getting dinner now, and screaming out the joyful news to everyone within hearing distance.